Woolsey

Daniel Woolsey

Neptune Rising

NEPTUNE RISING

Songs and Tales of the Undersea Folk

Jane Yolen

ILLUSTRATED BY

David Wiesner

PHILOMEL BOOKS   NEW YORK

ACKNOWLEDGMENTS

"The Undine," "Sule Skerry," "The River Maid," "The Lady and the Merman"
and "Corridors of the Sea" first appeared (sometimes in slightly altered form) in
The Magazine of Fantasy and Science Fiction. "The Lady and the Merman"
appeared in *The Hundredth Dove & Other Tales,* © 1977 by Jane Yolen, published
by Thomas Y. Crowell Company and is reprinted here by their kind permission.
"Greyling" is published as a separate picture book by Philomel Books, © 1968
by Jane Yolen. The poem "The Merman in Love" appeared in *Elsewhere,* Vol. 1,
published by Ace Books. The poem "The Selchie's Midnight Song" appeared in
Star*Line, the official publication of the Science Fiction Poetry Association.
The poem "Neptune Rising" appeared (in slightly altered form) in *The Magazine
of Fantasy and Science Fiction.*

Library of Congress Cataloging in Publication Data

Yolen, Jane. Neptune rising.

Summary: A collection of stories and poems
which feature merfolk.

1. Mermaids—Juvenile fiction.   2. Mermaids—
Juvenile poetry.   3. Children's stories, American.
4. Children's poetry, American.   [1. Mermaids—
Fiction.   2. Mermen—Fiction.   3. Mermaids—Poetry.
4. Mermen—Poetry.   5. Short stories.   6. American
poetry.]   I. Wiesner, David, ill.   II. Title.
PZ7.Y78Ne   [Fic]   82-5281
ISBN 0-399-20918-2   AACR2

For the Boks—Gordon and Pat
For the Dildines—John and Ginny
For the Fermans—Ed and Audrey
And for Robin McKinley

They feed the fantasy.

Contents

Neptune Rising

Introduction

Merfolk, many of the old tales tell us, have no tongues. That would make talking somewhat difficult for them. Fish have no tongues either. So I expect merfolk converse with their neighbors in a hand-wagging, tail-wiggling way, like fish. Yet merfolk are also amphibious air-breathers, who often sit on rocks or on the shore and sing their wordless songs.

There are hundreds of tales about such folk in the annals of world literature. In tale after tale we learn about their lost or misbegotten love affairs with humans: mermaids pining for princes, undines rejected by dukes, selchies stolen by fishermen for wives, the red-nosed merrow hauling off village maids. Or we hear about the power of the sea-gods—smelly old Proteus who could change shapes, for example. We read of King Manannan MacLir of Ireland leaving the Emerald Isle in a fit of pique, his misty cloak wrapped about his insubstantial body, repairing to the Isle of Man. Neptune/Poseidon with his trident, calling up tidal waves. Or the sea goddess Ran boiling up storms in her underwater caldron.

Why are there so many stories of the seafolk? Because the sea is around us and in us. Because we live on a planet that is mostly water. Because we begin our own lives floating for nine months in a watery sac. Because we live out our years in bodies that are more than 90% water. How could we humans do otherwise than think and dream and tell of the sea?

I grew up near various bodies of water. Born in New York, I lived almost thirteen years within easy walking distance of the Hudson River. Another part of my childhood was spent with my grandparents in Hampton Roads, Virginia, on the shore of Chesapeake Bay. And then I grew up the rest of the way in Westport, Connecticut, where the Long Island Sound pretends it is the Atlantic Ocean with varying degrees of success. I have also lived on the New England coast, crossed the Atlantic twice in boats, snorkeled in the Bay of Eilat, floated in the Dead Sea, waded near Worms Head in Wales, and dipped in the Pacific both in California and Washington State. Now I have an uneasy truce with the Connecticut River that flows not far from my farm. Within living memory (though not mine), its waters have flooded almost up to the farmhouse door. So I know a little about water. Perhaps that is why I have always been attracted to the lore and fantasy of the merfolk.

How true are the stories of the water spirits? Many people find it hard to put them all aside as mere fictions. For example, I know that in parts of the British Isles and also in some communities in Maryland, people still toss coins over the sides of their boats to propitiate the gods of the ocean. They call it "buying the sea." And I have a friend in Maine, a sailor-singer, who swears he knows a man who met a selchie once. My next door neighbor's little boy Jonathan has webbed toes.

And in a back-alley store in Greenwich, England, in 1979 I saw the mummified remains of a Malaysian merman. It was in a brass and glass case and the price tag said 300 pounds, about 600 American dollars then. Luckily it was already sold. But I took colored snapshots of it. I keep one over my desk as I write.

Those are some of the reasons I write about the sea and its denizens—its *magical* denizens. As a final note, it may interest some readers to know that I was born under Aquarius—a water sign. For my own part, I believe that to be only an accident of birth having more to do with my parents and their activities than with me. I do not think of myself primarily as an Aquarian, but as a poet and storyteller, seeking always the sources of the ancient magic and power—these may, however, be accessible only to those creatures of legend and fantasy, the mermaids, the sirens:

High on the rock, above the waves,
Coaxing the sailors to water-filled graves,
The siren sings her solo part.

Neither the rhythm nor yet the sound
Are the waters in which each hearer is drowned
As testimony to her art.

She sings far more than a sailor can hear.
He listens once with a cynical ear
And once with an innocent heart.

Poets and writers desire such skill:
That sirenlike we work our will
On every reader's ear and heart.

—Jane Yolen
Phoenix Farm
Hatfield, Massachusetts

Neptune Rising

Up through the blue-green furrow
as sturdy as spikes
of new grass
the three tines poke;
then the long shaft,
and around the haft
a hand.
The fingers are pale green,
the color of sea-foam,
and the webbings between them
gray as storm air.
Green veins
run rivulets
down the wrist
where rapid as a minnow
a pulse darts.

Close your eyes, landsman.
There is none
save seafolk
who can safely look
at Neptune rising.

The Lady
and the Merman

Once in a house overlooking the cold northern sea a baby was born. She was so plain, her father, a sea captain, remarked on it.

"She shall be a burden," he said. "She shall be on our hands forever." Then, without another glance at the child, he sailed off on his great ship.

His wife, who had longed to please him, was so hurt by his complaint that she soon died of it. Between one voyage and the next, she was gone.

When the captain came home and found this out, he was so enraged, he never spoke of his wife again. In this way he convinced himself that her loss was nothing.

But the girl lived and grew as if to spite her father. She

looked little like her dead mother but instead had the captain's face set round with mouse-brown curls. Yet as plain as her face was, her heart was not. She loved her father, but was not loved in return.

And still the captain remarked on her looks. He said at every meeting, "God must have wanted me cursed to give me such a child. No one will have her. She shall never be wed. She shall be with me forever." So he called her Borne, for she was his burden.

Borne grew into a lady, and only once gave a sign of this hurt.

"Father," she said one day when he was newly returned from the sea, "what can I do to heal this wound between us?"

He looked away from her, for he could not bear to see his own face mocked in hers, and spoke to the cold stone floor. "There is nothing between us, Daughter," he said. "But if there were, I would say, *Salt for such wounds.*"

"Salt?" Borne asked, surprised for she knew the sting of it.

"A sailor's balm," he said. "The salt of tears or the salt of sweat or the final salt of the sea." Then he turned from her and was gone next day to the farthest port he knew of, and in this way he cleansed his heart.

After this, Borne never spoke again of the hurt. Instead, she carried it silently like a dagger inside. For the salt of tears did not salve her, so she turned instead to work. She baked bread in her ovens for the poor, she nursed the sick, she held the hands of the sea widows. But always, late in the evening, she walked on the shore looking and longing for a sight of her father's sail. Only, less and less often did he return from the sea.

One evening, tired from the work of the day, Borne felt faint as she walked on the strand. Finding a rock half in and half out of the water, she climbed upon it to rest. She spread her skirts about her, and in the dusk they lay like great gray waves.

How long she sat there, still as the rock, she did not know. But a strange, pale moon came up. And as it rose, so too rose the little creatures of the deep. They leaped free for a moment of the pull of the tide. And last of all, up from the depths, came the merman.

He rose out of the crest of the wave, sea-foam crowning his green-black hair. His hands were raised high above him and the webbings of his fingers were as colorless as air. In the moonlight he seemed to stand upon his tail. Then, with a flick of it, he was gone, gone back to the deeps. He thought no one had remarked his dive.

But Borne had. So silent and still, she saw it all, his beauty and his power. She saw him and loved him, though she loved the fish half of him more. It was all she could dare.

She could not tell what she felt to a soul, for she had no one who cared about her feelings. Instead she forsook her work and walked by the sea both morning and night. Yet strange to say, she never once looked for her father's sail.

That is why her father returned one day without her knowing it. He watched her through slotted eyes as she paced the shore, for he would not look straight upon her. At last he went to her and said, "Be done with it. Whatever ails you, give it over." For even he could see *this* wound.

Borne looked up at him, her eyes shimmering with small seas. Grateful even for this attention, she answered, "Yes, Father, you are right. I must be done with it."

The captain turned and left her then, for his food was growing cold. But Borne went directly to the place where the waves were creeping onto the shore. She called out in a low voice, "Come up. Come up and be my love."

There was no answer except the shrieking laughter of the birds as they dove into the sea.

So she took a stick and wrote the same words upon the sand for the merman to see should he ever return. Only, as she watched, the creeping tide erased her words one by one by one. Soon there was nothing left of her cry on that shining strand.

So Borne sat herself down on the rock to weep. And each tear was an ocean.

But the words were not lost. Each syllable washed from the

beach was carried below, down, down, down to the deeps of the cool, inviting sea. And there, below on his coral bed, the merman saw her words and came.

He was all day swimming up to her. He was half the night seeking that particular strand. But when he came, cresting the currents, he surfaced with a mighty splash below Borne's rock.

The moon shone down on the two, she a grave shadow perched upon a stone and he all motion and light.

Borne reached down with her white hands and he caught them in his. It was the only touch she could remember. She smiled to see the webs stretched taut between his fingers. He laughed to see hers webless, thin, and small. One great pull between them and he was up by her side. Even in the dark, she could see his eyes on her under the phosphorescence of his hair.

He sat all night by her. And Borne loved the man of him as well as the fish, then, for in the silent night it was all one.

Then, before the sun could rise, she dropped her hands on his chest. "Can you love me?" she dared to ask at last.

But the merman had no tongue to tell her above the waves. He could only speak below the water with his hands, a soft murmuration. So, wordlessly, he stared into her eyes and pointed to the sea.

Then, with the sun just rising beyond the rim of the world, he turned, dove arrow-slim into a wave, and was gone.

Gathering her skirts, now heavy with ocean spray and tears, Borne stood up. She cast but one glance at the shore and her father's house beyond. Then she dove after the merman into the sea.

The sea put bubble jewels in her hair and spread her skirts about her like a scallop shell. Tiny colored fish swam in between her fingers. The water cast her face in silver and all the sea was reflected in her eyes.

She was beautiful for the first time. And for the last.

Old King Lir

Old King Lir,
the Irish sea-god
riding the Celtic waves,
believed his reign
would last
as long as a coastline.
He may have been
a god,
but he forgot
that men
and women,
being only human,
have the tools
to reshape the shore,
and their memories
are as erasable
as the footprints
of dunlin
scratched upon the sand.

The Undine

Aqua est mutabilis. Water is changeable, female, mutable. The gods of the sea are male, but the sea herself female. Beautiful. Restless. Changing. So the prince thought as he stared over the waves, the furrows becoming mountains, the mountains tumbling down into troughs. Female into male, male into female.

He pushed his scarlet hat to the back of his head because the feather tickled his cheek. Beautiful women were in his thoughts all the time, as delicately bothersome as the feather on his skin. Flickering, always flickering, on the edge of thought. He could no more stop thinking of them than stop the tides. He was to be married within a week.

He had never met his bride; that was not the pattern of the

courtship of royalty. But he had seen a portrait of her, a minia-
ture done by a painter whose pockets were even now lined with
gold from the girl's father. Such paintings told nothing truly,
not even the color of one's hair. His own portrait, sent in return,
showed a handsome youth with yellow curls, though in fact his
hair was more the color of a sparrow's belly, buffy and streaked.
The lies of kings are lightly told.

"I will not mind," he thought to himself. "I will not mind if
she is less than beautiful, as long as she is not *too* changeable. As
long as she is not under the water sign." He longed for stability
even as he sought change, an impossible pairing, but a prince's
wish.

A messenger arrived late that night who was one of his own.
Under the cover of darkness the messenger confided, "It is
worse than we thought, my lord. She has a face the very map of
disease, with the pox having carved out the central cities. Her
nose is mountainous, her chin the gift of ancestors. A castle
could be built upon that promontory."

The prince sighed and dismissed the news-bringer. Then he
began to pace the castle battlements, staring out across the cren-
ellations to the sea beyond. His father's father had built wisely;
one face of the castle was always turned toward the ocean. It
was a palace for sea-lovers and every room was full of the sound
of waves.

The prince leaned out over the wall and breathed in the salt spray. A wife whose face put a mountain range to shame. How could he—who loved the seascape, who loved beauty in women above all things—abide it? He longed suddenly for an ending, a sea change from his situation, but he had neither the heart for it nor the imagination. Princes are not bred to it. He sighed again.

It was the sigh that did it. It reeled out as eagerly as a fisherman's line and cast itself into the sea. What woman can resist the sound of a man's sigh? He had caught many maidens on it, many young matrons as well. But this time it was the daughter of a sea-king who was caught on *that* hook.

She rose to his bait and sang him back his sigh.

Now it must be remembered that the songs of mermaids have a charm compounded of water and air, the signs of impermanence. That is both their beauty and their danger. Many men have been caught, gaffed, reeled under and drowned by the lure of that song.

Rising out of the waves only to the edge of her waist—for she knew full well how the sight of a fish tail affects mortal men—the mermaid allowed the prince to gaze at her shell-like breasts, her pearly skin, the phosphorescence of her hair. She held a webbed hand over her mouth, her fingers as slim as the ribs of a fan. Then she pulled her hand away, displaying her smile. She was well trained in the arts of seduction, as was he. Royalty requires it.

The prince leaned out over the castle wall, his feet on the land, but his arms and head over the water. And thus, as amphibious as she, he promised himself to her, though he was not his own to give. It was a promise as mutable as water—for the promises of princes are lightly given.

We have all been warned of such bargains. Still that promise worked its own kind of magic and the undine rose from the waves on legs, her scales washed away by the prince's rote of love. But magic has consequences, as any magic-maker knows. The undine's new legs bit like knife points into her waist but she smiled and walked gingerly ashore.

The prince ran down to greet her, leaving bootmarks in the sand. If he had asked, she would have even danced before him and never minded the pain. Some women believe lies—even the ones they tell themselves. Or, perhaps, especially those.

The undine put her hand in his, and he shivered at her touch. Her hand was cold and slippery as a fish; the webbing between her fingers pulsed strangely against his skin. There was a strong sea scent about her, like tuna or like crab. But her chin and nose were small, and her eyes as blue as lagoons, and fathomless. He smiled his watery promise at her and gestured toward his room. He did not speak, knowing that mermaids have no tongues, forgetting in his human way that they have ears. Still, in love, gesture can be enough.

She followed him, knife upon knife, and smiling.

The prince took her to his room by a hidden route, the steps up to it smoothed by the passage of many dainty feet. But for the undine each step up was another gash in her side. She gasped and he asked her why.

"It is nothing," she signed with one hand, holding her waist with the other. Her mouth was open, gulping in the air, and she was momentarily as ugly as any fish. But the moment passed.

He did not ask again. Some men believe lies—especially if it is to their convenience to do so.

His room was like a ship's cabin, the waves always knocking at the walls. He locked the door behind them and turned toward her. She did not ask for ceremony. His touch was enough, rougher on her skin than the ocean. She enjoyed the novelty of it. She enjoyed his bed, heavy with humanity. Lying on it, her knife legs no longer ached.

Her touch on him was water-smooth and soothing. He forgot his impending marriage. He was always able to forget in this manner.

The week ticked away as inexorably as a gold watch and the monstrous royal bride embarked across the waves. She resembled a warship, rough-hewn and wooden, with a mighty prow.

In her wake was an armada of guardsmen. Her attendants, noisy as sea gulls, knocked on his door. The bride was ready. The prince was obliged to attend her; the undine he left behind.

"I love you. My love is an ocean," he whispered into her seashell ears before he left.

The undine knew such an ocean was changeable. It was subject to tides. Hers was at an ebb. She no longer trusted his mutable vows. As soon as the door shut, she left the bed. The knife points were as sharp as if newly honed. The mirror on the wall did not reflect her beauty; it showed only a watery shadow, changing and shifting, as she passed.

The salt smell of the ocean, sharp and steady, called to her from the window. Looking out, she saw her sisters, the waves, beckoning her with their white arms. She could even hear the rough neighing of the horses of the sea. She left two mermaid tears, crystals with a bit of salt embedded in them, on his pillow. Then, painfully, she climbed up onto the windowsill and flung herself back at the sea.

It opened to her, gathered her in, washed her clean.

The prince found the crystals and made them into earbobs for his ugly wife. They did not improve her looks. But when he became king she proved a strong, stable queen for him, and ruled the kingdom on her own. She gave him much line, she played him like a fish. She swore to him that she did not mind his many affairs or that he spoke in his sleep of undines.

Thus she swore, and he believed her. But the lies of kings—
and of queens—are not *always* lightly told.

Undine

It is a sad tale,
the one they tell,
of Undine
the changeling,
Undine
who took on legs
to walk the land
and dance
on those ungainly stalks
before a prince
of the earthfolk.
He betrayed her;
they always do,
the landsmen.
Her arms around him
meant little more
than a finger of foam
curled round his ankle.

Her lips on his
he thought cold,
brief and cold
as the touch of a wave.
He betrayed her,
they always do,
left her to find
her way back home
over thousands of land miles,
the only salt her tears,
and she as helpless
as a piece of featherweed
tossed broken onto the shore.

Greyling

Once on a time when wishes were aplenty, a fisherman and his wife lived by the side of the sea. All that they ate came out of the sea. Their hut was covered with the finest mosses that kept them cool in the summer and warm in the winter. And there was nothing they needed or wanted except a child.

Each morning, when the moon touched down behind the water and the sun rose up behind the plains, the wife would say to the fisherman, "You have your boat and your nets and your lines. But I have no baby to hold in my arms." And again, in the evening, it was the same. She would weep and wail and rock the cradle that stood by the hearth. But year in and year out the cradle stayed empty.

Now the fisherman was also sad that they had no child. But he kept his sorrow to himself so that his wife would not know his grief and thus double her own. Indeed, he would leave the hut each morning with a breath of song and return each night with a whistle on his lips. His nets were full but his heart was empty, yet he never told his wife.

One sunny day, when the beach was a tan thread spun between sea and plain, the fisherman as usual went down to his boat. But this day he found a small grey seal stranded on the sandbar, crying for its own.

The fisherman looked up the beach and down. He looked in front of him and behind. And he looked to the town on the great grey cliffs that sheared off into the sea. But there were no other seals in sight.

So he shrugged his shoulders and took off his shirt. Then he dipped it into the water and wrapped the seal pup carefully in its folds.

"You have no father and you have no mother," he said. "And I have no child. So you shall come home with me."

And the fisherman did no fishing that day but brought the seal pup, wrapped in his shirt, straight home to his wife.

When she saw him coming home early with no shirt on, the fisherman's wife ran out of the hut, fear riding in her heart. Then she looked wonderingly at the bundle which he held in his arms.

"It is nothing," he said, "but a seal pup I found stranded in the shallows and longing for its own. I thought we could give it love and care until it is old enough to seek its kin."

The fisherman's wife nodded and took the bundle. Then she uncovered the wrapping and gave a loud cry. "Nothing!" she said. "You call this nothing?"

The fisherman looked. Instead of a seal lying in the folds, there was a strange child with great grey eyes and silvery grey hair, smiling up at him.

The fisherman wrung his hands. "It is a selchie," he cried. "I have heard of them. They are men upon the land and seals in the sea. I thought it was but a tale."

"Then he shall remain a man upon the land," said the fisherman's wife, clasping the child in her arms, "for I shall never let him return to the sea."

"Never," agreed the fisherman, for he knew how his wife had wanted a child. And in his secret heart, he wanted one, too. Yet he felt, somehow, it was wrong.

"We shall call him Greyling," said the fisherman's wife, "for his eyes and hair are the color of a storm-coming sky. Greyling, though he has brought sunlight into our home."

And though they still lived by the side of the water in a hut covered with mosses that kept them warm in the winter and cool in the summer, the boy Greyling was never allowed into the sea.

He grew from a child to a lad. He grew from a lad to a young man. He gathered driftwood for his mother's hearth and searched the tide pools for shells for her mantel. He mended his father's nets and tended his father's boat. But though he often stood by the shore or high in the town on the great grey cliffs, looking and longing and grieving his heart for what he did not really know, he never went into the sea.

Then one wind-wailing morning just fifteen years from the day that Greyling had been found, a great storm blew up suddenly in the North. It was such a storm as had never been seen before: the sky turned nearly black and even the fish had trouble swimming. The wind pushed huge waves onto the shore. The waters gobbled up the little hut on the beach. And Greyling and the fisherman's wife were forced to flee to the town high on the great grey cliffs. There they looked down at the roiling, boiling sea. Far from shore they spied the fisherman's boat, its sails flapping like the wings of a wounded gull. And clinging to the broken mast was the fisherman himself, sinking deeper with every wave.

The fisherman's wife gave a terrible cry. "Will no one save him?" she called to the people of the town who had gathered on the edge of the cliff. "Will no one save my own dear husband who is all of life to me?"

But the townsmen looked away. There was no man there who dared risk his life in that sea, even to save a drowning soul.

"Will no one at all save him?" she cried out again.

"Let the boy go," said one old man, pointing at Greyling with his stick. "He looks strong enough."

But the fisherman's wife clasped Greyling in her arms and held his ears with her hands. She did not want him to go into the sea. She was afraid he would never return.

"Will no one save my own dear heart?" cried the fisherman's wife for a third and last time.

But shaking their heads, the people of the town edged to their houses and shut their doors and locked their windows and set their backs to the ocean and their faces to the fires that glowed in every hearth.

"I will save him, Mother," cried Greyling, "or die as I try."

And before she could tell him no, he broke from her grasp and dived from the top of the great cliffs, down, down, down into the tumbling sea.

"He will surely sink," whispered the women as they ran from their warm fires to watch.

"He will certainly drown," called the men as they took down their spyglasses from the shelves.

They gathered on the cliffs and watched the boy dive down into the sea.

As Greyling disappeared beneath the waves, little fingers of foam tore at his clothes. They snatched his shirt and his pants and his shoes and sent them bubbling away to the shore. And as Greyling went deeper beneath the waves, even his skin seemed to slough off till he swam, free at last, in the sleek grey coat of a great grey seal.

The selchie had returned to the sea.

But the people of the town did not see this. All they saw was the diving boy disappearing under the waves and then, farther out, a large seal swimming toward the boat that wallowed in the sea. The sleek grey seal, with no effort at all, eased the fisherman to the shore though the waves were wild and bright with foam. And then, with a final salute, it turned its back on the land and headed joyously out to sea.

The fisherman's wife hurried down to the sand. And behind her followed the people of the town. They searched up the beach and down, but they did not find the boy.

"A brave son," said the men when they found his shirt, for they thought he was certainly drowned.

"A very brave son," said the women when they found his shoes, for they thought him lost for sure.

"Has he really gone?" asked the fisherman's wife of her husband when at last they were alone.

"Yes, quite gone," the fisherman said to her. "Gone where his heart calls, gone to the great wide sea. And though my heart grieves at his leaving, it tells me this way is best."

The fisherman's wife sighed. And then she cried. But at last she agreed that, perhaps, it was best. "For he is both man and seal," she said. "And though we cared for him for a while, now he must care for himself." And she never cried again.

So once more they lived alone by the side of the sea in a new little hut which was covered with mosses to keep them warm in the winter and cool in the summer.

Yet, once a year, a great grey seal is seen at night near the fisherman's home. And the people in town talk of it, and wonder. But seals do come to the shore and men do go to the sea; and so the townfolk do not dwell upon it very long.

But it is no ordinary seal. It is Greyling himself come home—come to tell his parents tales of the lands that lie far beyond the waters, and to sing them songs of the wonders that lie far beneath the sea.

Ballad of the White Seal Maid

The fisherman sits alone on the land,
His hands are his craft, his boat is his art,
The fisherman sits alone on the land,
A rock, a rock in his heart.

The selchie maid swims alone in the bay,
Her eyes are the seal's, her heart is the sea,
The selchie maid swims alone through the bay,
A white seal maid is she.

She comes to the shore and sheds her seal skin,
She dances on sand and under the moon,
Her hair falls in waves all down her white skin,
Only the seals hear the tune.

The fisherman stands and takes up her skin,
Staking his claim to a wife from the sea,
He raises his hand and holds up the skin,
"Now you must come home with me."

Weeping she goes and weeping she stays,
Her hands are her craft, her babes are her art,
A year and a year and a year more she stays,
A rock, a rock in her heart.

But what is this hid in the fisherman's bag?
It smells of the ocean, it feels like the sea,
A bony-white seal skin closed up in the bag,
And never a tear more sheds she.

"Good-bye to the house and good-bye to the shore,
Good-bye to the babes that I never could claim.
But never a thought to the man left on shore,
For selchie's my nature and name."

She puts on the skin and dives back in the sea,
The fisherman's cry falls on water-deaf ears.
She swims in her seal skin far out to the sea.
The fisherman drowns in his tears.

Sule Skerry

Mairi rowed the coracle with quick, angry strokes, watching the rocky shoreline and the little town of Caith perched on its edge recede. She wished she could make her anger disappear as easily. She was sixteen, after all, and no longer a child. The soldiers whistled at her, even in her school uniform, when she walked to and from the Academy. And wasn't Harry Stones, who was five years older than she and a lieutenant in the RAF, a tail gunner, mad about her? Given a little time, he might have asked her dad for her hand, though she was too young yet, a schoolgirl. Whenever he came to visit, he brought her something. Once even a box of chocolates, though they were very dear.

But to be sent away from London for safekeeping like a baby, to her gran's house, to this desolate, isolated Scottish sea town because of a few German raids—it was demeaning. She could have helped, could have at least cooked and taken care of the flat for her father now that the help had all gone off to war jobs. She had wanted to be there in case a bomb *did* fall, so she could race out and help evacuate all the poor unfortunates, maybe even win a medal, and wouldn't Jenny Eivensley look green then. But he had sent her off, her dad, and Harry had agreed, even though it meant they couldn't see each other very often. It was not in the least fair.

She pulled again on the oars. The little skin boat tended to wallow and needed extra bullying. It wasn't built like a proper British rowboat. It was roundish, shaped more like a turtle shell than a ship. Mairi hated it, hated all of the things in Caith. She knew she should have been in London helping rather than fooling about in a coracle. She pulled on the oars and the boat shot ahead.

The thing about rowing, she reminded herself, was that you watched where you had been, not where you were heading. She could see the town, with its crown of mewing seabirds, disappear from sight. Her destination did not matter. It was all ocean anyway—cold, uninviting, opaque; a dark-green mirror that reflected nothing. And now there was ocean behind as well as ahead, for the shore had thinned out to an invisible line.

Suddenly, without warning, the coracle fetched up against a
rock, a series of water-smoothed amphibious mounds that
loomed up out of the sea. Only at the bump did Mairi turn and
look. Out of the corner of her eye she saw a quick scurry of
something large and gray and furry on the far side of the rocks.
She heard a splash.

"Oh," she said out loud. "A seal!"

The prospect of having come upon a seal rookery was
enough to make her leap incautiously from the coracle onto the
rock, almost losing the boat in her eagerness. But her anger was
forgotten. She leaned over and pulled the little boat out of the
water, scraping its hull along the gray granite. Then she upended
the coracle and left it to dry, looking for all the world like a
great dozing tortoise drying in the hazy sun.

Mairi shrugged out of her mackintosh and draped it on the
rock next to the boat. Then, snugging the watch cap down over
her curls and pulling the bulky fisherman's sweater over her slim
hips, she began her ascent.

The rocks were covered with a strange purple-gray lichen that
was both soft and slippery. Mairi fell once, bruising her right
knee without ripping her trousers. She cursed softly, trying out
swearwords that she had never been allowed to use at home or
in Gran's great house back on shore. Then she started up again,
on her hands and knees, more carefully now, and at last gained

the high point on the rocks after a furious minute of climbing that went backwards and sideways almost as often as it went up. The top of the gray rocks was free of the lichen and she was able to stand up, feeling safe, and look around.

She could not see Caith, with its little, watchful, wind-scored houses lined up like a homefront army to face the oncoming tides in the firth, with Gran's grand house standing on one side, the sergeant-major. She could not even see the hills behind, where cliffs hunched like the bleached fossils of some enormous prehistoric ocean beast washed ashore. All that she could see was the unbroken sea, blue and black and green and gray, with patterns of color that shifted as quickly as the pieces in a child's kaleidoscope. Gray-white foam skipped across wave tops, then tumbled down and fractured into bubbles that popped erratically, leaving nothing but a grayish scum that soon became shiny water again. She thought she saw one or two dark seal heads in the troughs of the waves, but they never came close enough for her to count. And overhead the sky was lowering, a color so dirty that it would have made even the bravest sailor long for shore. There was a storm coming, and Mairi guessed she should leave.

She shivered, and suddenly knew where she was. These rocks were the infamous Sule Skerry rocks that Gran's cook had told her about.

"Some may call it a rookery," Cook had said one morning when Mairi had visited with her in the dark kitchen. Cook's cooking was awful—dry, bland, and unvaried. But at least she knew stories and always imparted them with an intensity that made even the strangest of them seem real. "Aye, some may call it a rookery. But us from Caith, we know. It be the home of the selchies, who are men on land and seals in the sea. And the Great Selchie himself lives on that rock. Tall he is. And covered with a seal skin when he tumbles in the waves. But he is a man for all that. And no maiden who goes to Sule Skerry returns the same."

She had hummed a bit of an old song, then, with a haunting melody that Mairi, for all her music training at school, could not repeat. But the words of the song, some of them, had stuck with her:

> *An earthly nourrice sits and sings,*
> *And aye she sings, "Ba, lily wean!*
> *Little ken I my bairn's father,*
> *Far less the land that he staps in."*
>
> *Then ane arose at her bed-fit,*
> *An a grumly guest I'm sure was he:*
> *"Here am I, thy bairn's father,*
> *Although I be not comelie.*

49

I am a man upon the land,
I am a selchie in the sea
And when I'm far frae ev'ry strand
My dwelling is in Sule Skerry."

A warning tale, Mairi thought. A bogeyman story to keep fool-ish girls safe at home. She smiled. She was a Londoner, after all, not a silly Scots girl who'd never been out of her own town.

And then she heard a strange sound, almost like an echo of the music of Cook's song, from the backside of the rocks. At first she thought it was the sound of wind against water, the sound she heard continuously at Gran's home where every room rustled with the music of the sea. But this was different some-how, a sweet, low throbbing, part moan and part chant. Without knowing the why of it, only feeling a longing brought on by the wordless song, and excusing it as seeking to solve a mystery, she went looking for the source of the song. The rock face was smooth on this side, dry, without the slippery, somber lichen; and the water was calmer so it did not splash up spray. Mairi continued down the side, the tune reeling her in effortlessly.

Near the waterline was a cave opening into the west face of the rock, a man-sized opening as black and uninviting as a col-liers' pit. But she took a deep, quick breath, and went in.

Much to her surprise, the inside of the cave glowed with an incandescent blue-green light that seemed to come from the cave walls themselves. Darker pockets of light illuminated the concave sections of the wall. Pieces of seaweed caught in these niches gave the appearance of household gods.

Mairi could scarcely breathe. Any loud sound seemed sacrilegious. Her breath itself was a violation.

And then she heard the moan-song again, so loud that it seemed to fill the entire cave. It swelled upward like a wave, then broke off in a bubbling sigh.

Mairi walked in slowly, not daring to touch the cave walls in case she should mar the perfection of the color, yet fearing that she might fall, for the floor of the cave was slippery with scattered puddles of water. Slowly, one foot in front of the other, she explored the cave. In the blue-green light, her sweater and skin seemed to take on an underwater tinge as if she had been transformed into a mermaid.

And then the cave ended, tapering off to a rounded apse with a kind of stone altar the height of a bed. There was something dark lying on the rock slab. Fearfully, Mairi inched toward it and when she got close, the dark thing heaved up slightly and spoke to her in a strange guttural tongue. At first Mairi thought it was a seal, a wounded seal, but then she saw it was a man huddled under a sealskin coat. He suddenly lay back, feverish and shuddering, and she saw the beads of dried blood that circled his head like a crown.

Without thinking, Mairi moved closer and put her hand on

his forehead, expecting it to burn with temperature, but he was cold and damp and slippery to the touch. Then he opened his eyes and they were the same blue-green color as the walls, as the underside of a wave. She wondered for a moment if he were blind, for there seemed to be no pupil in those eyes. Then he closed the lids and smiled at her, whispering in that same unknown tongue.

"Never mind, never mind, I'll get help," whispered Mairi. He might be a fisherman from the town or an RAF man shot down on a mission. She looked at his closed-down face. Here, at last, was her way to aid the war effort. "Lie still. First I'll see to your wounds. They taught us first aid at school."

She examined his forehead under the slate-gray hair, and saw that the terrible wound that had been there was now closed and appeared to be healing, though bloody and seamed with scabs. But when she started to slip the sealskin coat down to examine him for other wounds, she was shocked to discover he had no clothes on under it. No clothes at all.

She hesitated then. Except for the statues in the museum, Mairi had never seen a man naked. Not even in the first aid books. But what if he were *hurt unto death*? The fearsome poetry of the old phrase decided her. She inched back the sealskin covering as gently as she could.

He did not move except for the rise and fall of his chest. His body was covered with fine hairs, gray as the hair on his head. He had broad, powerful shoulders and slim, tapering hips. The skin on his hands was strangely wrinkled as if he had been under water too long. She realized with a start that he was quite, quite beautiful—but alien. As her grandmother often said, "Men are queer creatures, so different from us, child. And someday you will know it."

Then his eyes opened again and she could not look away from them. He smiled, opened his mouth, and began to speak, to chant really. Mairi bent down over him and he opened his arms to her, the gray webbing between his fingers pulsing strongly. And without willing it, she covered his mouth with hers. All the sea was in that kiss, cold and vast and perilous. It drew her in till she thought she would faint with it, with his tongue darting around hers as quick as a minnow. And then his arms encircled her and he was as strong as the tide. She felt only the briefest of pain, and a kind of drowning, and she let the land go.

When Mairi awoke, she was sitting on the stone floor of the cavern, and cold, bone-chilling cold. She shivered and pushed her hand across her cheeks. They were wet, though whether with tears or from the damp air she could not say.

Above her, on the stone bed, the wounded man breathed

raggedly. Occasionally he let out a moan. Mairi stood and looked down at him. His flesh was pale, wan, almost translucent. She put her hand on his shoulder but he did not move. She wondered if she had fallen and hit her head, if she had dreamed what had happened.

"Help. I must get help for him," she thought. She covered him again with the coat and made her way back to the cave mouth. Her entire body ached and she decided she must have fallen and blacked out.

The threatening storm had not yet struck, but the dark slant of rain against the horizon was closer still. Mairi scrambled along the rocks to where the coracle waited. She put on her mac, then heaved the boat over and into the water and slipped in, getting only her boots wet.

It was more difficult rowing back, rowing against the tide. Waves broke over the bow of the little boat, and by the time she was within sight of the town, she was soaked to the skin. The stones of Sule Skerry were little more than gray wave tops then, and with one pull on the oars, they disappeared from sight. The port enfolded her, drew her in. She felt safe and lonely at once.

When Mairi reached the shore there was a knot of fishermen tending their boats. A few were still at work on the bright orange nets, folding them carefully in that quick, intricate pattern that only they seemed to know.

One man, in a blue watch cap, held up a large piece of tattered white cloth, an awning of silk. It seemed to draw the other men to him. He gestured with the silk and it billowed out as if capturing the coming storm.

Suddenly Mairi was horribly afraid. She broke into the circle of men. "Oh, please, please," she cried out, hearing the growing wail of wind in her voice. "There's a man on the rocks. He's hurt."

"The rocks?" The man with the silk stuffed it into his pocket, but a large fold of it hung down his side. "Which rocks?"

"Out there. Beyond the sight line. Where the seals stay," Mairi said.

"Whose child is she?" asked a man who still carried an orange net. He spoke as if she were too young to understand him or as if she were a foreigner.

"Old Mrs. Goodleigh's grandchild. The one with the English father," came an answer.

"Mavis' daughter, the one who became a nurse in London."

"Too good for Caith, then?"

Mairi was swirled about in their conversation.

"Please," she tried again.

"Suppose'n she means the Rocks?"

"Yes," begged Mairi. "The rocks out there. Sule Skerry."

"Hush, child. Must na say the name in sight of the sea," said the blue cap man.

"Toss it a coin, Jock," said the white silk man.

The man called Jock reached into his pocket and flung a coin out to the ocean. It skipped across the waves twice, then sank.

"That should quiet en. Now then, the Rocks you say?"

Mairi turned to the questioner. He had a face like a map, wrinkles marking the boundaries of nose and cheek. "Yes, sir," she said breathily.

"Aye, he might have fetched up there," said the white silk man, drawing it out of his pocket again for the others to see.

Did they know him, then? Mairi wondered.

"Should we leave him to the storm?" asked Jock.

"He might be one of ours," the map-faced man said.

They all nodded at that.

"He's sheltered," Mairi said suddenly. "In a cave. A grotto, like. It's all cast over with a blue and green light."

"Teched, she is. There's no grotto there," said blue cap.

"No blue and green light either," said the map-faced man, turning from her and speaking earnestly with his companions. "Even if he's one of them, he might tell us summat we need.

Our boys could use the knowledge. From that bit of parachute silk, it's hard to say which side he's on." He reached out and touched the white cloth with a gnarled finger.

"Aye, we'd best look for him."

"He won't be hard to find," Mairi began. "He's sick. Hurt. I touched him."

"What was he wearing then?" asked blue cap.

The wind had picked up and Mairi couldn't hear the question. "What?" she shouted.

"Wearing. *What was the fellow wearing?*"

Suddenly remembering that the man had been naked under the coat, she was silent.

"She doesn't know. Probably too scared to go close. Come on," said Jock.

The men pushed past her and dragged along two of the large six-man boats that fished the haaf banks. The waves were slapping angrily at the shore, gobbling up pieces of the sand and churning out pebbles at each retreat. Twelve men scrambled into the boats and headed out to sea, their oars flashing together.

Three men were left on shore, including the one holding the remnant of white silk. They stood staring out over the cold waters, their eyes squinted almost shut against the strange bright light that was running before the storm.

57

Mairi stood near them, but apart.

No one spoke.

It was a long half hour before the first of the boats leaped back toward them, across a wave, seconds ahead of the rain.

The second boat beached just as the storm broke, the men jumping out onto the sand and drawing the boat up behind them. A dark form was huddled against the stern.

Mairi tried to push through to get a close glimpse of the man, but blue cap spoke softly to her.

"Nay, nay girl, don't look. He's not what you would call a pretty sight. He pulled a gun on Jock and Jock took a rock to him."

But Mairi had seen enough. The man was dressed in a flier's suit, and a leather jacket with zippers. His blond hair was matted with blood.

"That's not the one I saw," she murmured. "Not the one I . . ."

"Found him lying on the rocks, just as the girl said. Down by the west side of the rocks," said Jock. "We threw his coins to the sea and bought our way home. Though I don't know that German coins buy much around here. Bloody Huns."

"What's a German flier doing this far west, I'd like to know," said map-face.

"Maybe he was trying for America," Jock answered, laughing sourly.

"Ask him. When he's fit to talk," said blue cap.

The man with the white silk wrapped it around the German's neck. The parachute shroud lines hung down the man's back. Head down, the German was marched between Jock and blue cap up the strand and onto the main street. The other men trailed behind.

With the rain soaking through her cap and running down her cheeks, Mairi took a step toward them. Then she turned away. She kicked slowly along the water's edge till she found the stone steps that led up to her gran's house. The sea pounded a steady reminder on her left, a basso continuo to the song that ran around in her head. The last three verses came to her slowly.

> *Now he has ta'en a purse of goud*
> *And he has put it upon her knee*
> *Sayin' "Gie to me my little young son*
> *An tak ye up thy nourrice-fee."*

She shivered and put her hands in her pockets to keep them warm. In one of the mac's deep pockets, her fingers felt something cold and rough to the touch. Reluctantly she drew it out. It was a coin, green and gold, slightly crusted, as if it had lain on the ocean bottom for some time. She had never seen it before and could only guess how it had gotten into her coat pocket. She closed her hand around the coin, so tightly a second coin was imprinted on her palm.

> An it shall pass on a summer's day
> When the sun shines het on every stane
> That I will tak my little young son
> An teach him for to swim his lane.
>
> An thu sall marry a proud gunner
> An a right proud gunner I'm sure he'll be.
> An the very first shot that ere he shoots
> He'll kill baith my young son and me.

Had it truly happened, or was it just some dream brought on by a fall? She felt again those cold, compelling hands on her, the movement of the webbings pulsing on her breasts; smelled again the briny odor of his breath. And if she *did* have that bairn, that child? Why, Harry Stones would *have* to marry her, then. Her father could not deny them that.

And laughing and crying at the same time, Mairi began to run up the stone steps. The sound of the sea followed her all the way home, part melody and part unending moan.

The Selchie's Midnight Song

The moon on my shoulder
Is no heavy burden,
The hide on my back
Is quite easy to bear,
The tumbling water
Does not halt my progress
    The man's hand on mine
    Is what I most fear.

The pup's mewling whimper,
The scream of the white gull,
The rattle of cowries
Washed up by the sea,
Are music that calls me
From landward to seaward.
    The cries in the cradle
    Mean nothing to me.

One Old Man, with Seals

The day was clear and sharp and fresh when I first heard the seals. They were crying, a symphony of calls. The bulls coughed a low bass. The pups had a mewing whimper, not unlike the cry of a human child. I heard them as I ran around the lighthouse, the slippery sands making my ritual laps more exercise than I needed, more than the doctor said a seventy-five-year-old woman should indulge in. Of course he didn't say it quite like that. Doctors never do. He said: "*A woman of your age* . . ." and left it for me to fill in the blanks. It was a physician's pathetically inept attempt at tact. Any lie told then would be mine, not his.

However, as much as doctors know about blood and bones,

they never do probe the secret recesses of the heart. And my heart told me that I was still twenty-five. Well, forty-five, anyway. And I had my own methods of gray liberation.

I had bought a lighthouse, abandoned as unsafe and no longer viable by the Coast Guard. (Much as I had been by the county library system. One abandoned and no longer viable children's librarian, greatly weathered and worth one gold watch, no more.) I spent a good part of my savings renovating, building bookcases and having a phone line brought in. And making sure the electricity would run my refrigerator, freezer, hi-fi, and TV set. I am a solitary, not a primitive, and my passion is the news. With in-town cable, I could have watched twenty-four hours a day. But in my lighthouse, news magazines and books of history took up the slack.

Used to a life of discipline and organization, I kept to a rigid schedule even though there was no one to impress with my dedication. But I always sang as I worked. As some obscure poet has written, "No faith can last that never sings." Up at daylight, a light breakfast while watching the morning newscasters, commercials a perfect time to scan *Newsweek* or *Time*. Then off for my morning run. Three laps seemed just right to get lungs and heart working. Then back inside to read until my nephew called. He is a classics scholar at the University and my favorite relative. I've marked him down in my will for all my books and subscriptions—and the lighthouse. The others will split the little bit of money I have left. Since I have been a collector of fine and rare history books for over fifty years, my nephew will be well off, though he doesn't know it yet.

The phone rings between ten and eleven every morning, and it is always Mike. He wants to be sure I'm still alive and kicking. The one time I had flu and was too sick to answer the phone, he was over like a shot in that funny lobster boat of his. I could hear him pounding up the stairs and shouting my name. He even had his friend, Dr. Lil Meyer, with him. A *real* doctor, he calls her, not his kind, "all letters and no learning."

They gave me plenty of juice and spent several nights, though it meant sleeping on the floor for both of them. But they didn't seem to mind. And when I was well again, they took off in the lobster boat, waving madly and leaving a wake as broad as a city sidewalk.

For a doctor, Lil Meyer wasn't too bad. She seemed to know about the heart. She said to me, whispered so Mike wouldn't hear her, just before she left, "You're sounder than any seventy-five-year-old I've ever met, Aunt Lyssa. I don't know if it's the singing or the running or the news. But whatever it is, just keep doing it. And Mike and I will keep tabs on you."

The day I heard the seals singing, I left off my laps and went investigating. It never does to leave a mystery unsolved at my

65

age. Curiosity alone would keep me awake, and I need my sleep. Besides, I knew that the only singing done on these shores recently was my own. Seals never came here, hadn't for at least as long as I had owned the lighthouse. And according to the records, which the Coast Guard had neglected to collect when they condemned the place, leaving me with a week-long feast of old news, there hadn't been any seals for the last 100 years. Oh, there had been plenty else—wrecks and flotsam. Wrackweed wound around the detritus of civilization: Dixie Cups, beer cans, pop bottles, and newsprint. And a small school of whales had beached themselves at the north tip of the beach in 1957 and had to be hauled off by an old whaling vessel, circa 1923, pressed into service. But no seals.

The lighthouse sits way out on a tip of land, some sixteen miles from town, and at high tide it is an island. There have been some minor skirmishes over calling it a wildlife preserve, but the closest the state has come to that has been to post some yellow signs that have weathered to the color of old mustard and are just as readable. The southeast shore is the milder shore, sheltered from the winds and battering tides. The little bay that runs between Lighthouse Point and the town of Tarryton-Across-the-Bay, as the early maps have it, is always filled with pleasure boats. By half May, the bigger yachts of the summer folk start to arrive, great white swans gliding serenely in while the smaller, colorful boats of the year-rounders squawk and gabble and gawk at them, darting about like so many squabbling mallards or grebes.

The singing of the seals came from the rougher northwest shore. So I headed that way, no longer jogging because it was a rocky run. If I slipped and fell, I might lie with a broken hip or arm for hours or days before Mike finally came out to find me. *If* he found me at all. So I picked my way carefully around the granite outcroppings.

I had only tried that northern route once or twice before. Even feeling twenty-five or forty-five, I found myself defeated by the amount of rock-climbing necessary to go the entire way. But I kept it up this time because after five minutes the seal song had become louder, more melodic, compelling. And, too, an incredible smell had found its way into my nose.

I say *found* because one of the sadder erosions of age has been a gradual loss of my sense of smell. Oh, really sharp odors eventually reach me, and I am still sensitive to the intense prickles of burned wood. But the subtle tracings of a good liqueur or the shadings of a wine's bouquet are beyond me. And recently, to my chagrin, I burned up my favorite teakettle because the whistle had failed and I didn't smell the metal melting until it was too late.

However, this must have been a powerful scent to have

reached me out near the ocean, with the salt air blowing at ten miles an hour. Not a really strong wind, as coastal winds go, but strong enough.

And so I followed my ear—and my nose.

They led me around one last big rock, about the size of a small Minke whale. And it was then I saw the seals. They were bunched together and singing their snuffling hymns. Lying in their midst was an incredibly dirty bum, asleep and snoring.

I almost turned back then, but the old man let out a groan. Only then did it occur to me what a bizarre picture it was. Here was a bearded patriarch of the seals—for they were quite unafraid of him—obviously sleeping off a monumental drunk. In fact I had no idea where he had gotten and consumed his liquor or how he had ever made it to that place, sixteen miles from the nearest town by land, and a long swim by sea. There was no boat to be seen. He lay as if dropped from above, one arm flung over a large bull seal which acted like a pup, snuggling close to him and pushing at his armpit with its nose.

At that I laughed out loud and the seals, startled by the noise, fled down the shingle toward the sea, humping their way across the rocks and pebbly beach to safety in the waves. But the old man did not move.

It was then that I wondered if he were not drunk but rather injured, flung out of the sea by the tide, another bit of flotsam on my beach. So I walked closer.

The smell was stronger, and I realized it was not the seals I had been smelling. It was the old man. After years of dealing with children in libraries—from babies to young adults—I had learned to identify a variety of smells, from feces to vomit to pot. And though my sense of smell was almost defunct, my memory was not. But that old man smelled of none of the things I could easily recognize, or of anything the land had to offer. He smelled of seals and salt and water, like a wreck that had long lain on the bottom of the ocean suddenly uncovered by a freak storm. He smelled of age, incredible age. I could literally smell the centuries on him. If I was seventy-five, he had to be four, no forty times that. That was fanciful of me. Ridiculous. But it was my immediate and overwhelming thought.

I bent over him to see if I could spot an injury, something I might reasonably deal with. His gray-white, matted hair was thin and lay over his scalp like the scribbles of a mad artist. His beard was braided with seaweed, and shells lay entangled in the briery locks. His fingernails were encrusted with dirt. Even the lines of his face were deeply etched with a greenish grime. But I saw no wounds.

His clothes were an archeological dig. Around his neck were the collars of at least twenty shirts. Obviously he put on one shirt and wore it until there was nothing left but the ring, then

simply donned another. His trousers were a similar ragbag of
colors and weaves, and only the weakness of waistbands had
kept him from having accumulated a lifetime supply. He was
barefoot. The nails on his toes were as yellow as jingleshells,
and so long they curled over each toe like a sheath.

He moaned again, and I touched him on the shoulder, hoping
to shake him awake. But when I touched him, his shoulder burst
into flames. Truly. Little fingers of fire spiked my palm. Spon-
taneous combustion was something I had only read about: a
heap of oily rags in a hot closet leading to fire. But his rags were
not oily, and the weather was a brisk 68 degrees, with a good
wind blowing.

I leaped back and screamed and he opened one eye.

The flames subsided, went out. He began to snore again.

The bull seals came out of the water and began a large, irreg-
ular circle around us. So I stood up and turned to face them.

"Shoo!" I said, taking off my watch cap. I wear it to keep my
ears warm when I run. "Shoo!" Flapping the cap at them and
stepping briskly forward, I challenged the bulls.

They broke circle and scattered, moving about a hundred feet
away in that awkward shuffling gait they have on land. Then
they turned and stared at me. The younger seals and the females
remained in the water, a watchful bobbing.

I went back to the old man. "Come on," I said. "I know

70

you're awake now. Be sensible. Tell me if anything hurts or aches. I'll help you if you need help. And if not—I'll just go away."

He opened the one eye again and cleared his throat. It sounded just like a bull seal's cough. But he said nothing.

I took a step closer and he opened his other eye. They were as blue as the ocean over white sand. Clear and clean, the only clean part of him.

I bent over to touch his shoulder again, and this time the material of his shirt began to smolder under my hand.

"That's a trick," I said. "Or hypnotism. Enough of that."

He smiled. And the smoldering ceased. Instead, his shoulder seemed to tumble under my hand, like waves, like torrents, like a full high tide. My hand and sleeve were suddenly wet; sloppily, thoroughly wet.

I clenched my teeth. Mike always said that New England spinsters are so full of righteous fortitude they might be mistaken for mules. And my forebears go back seven generations in Maine. Maybe I didn't understand what was happening, but that was no excuse for lack of discipline and not holding on. I held on.

The old man sighed.

Under my hand, the shoulder changed again, the material and then the flesh wriggling and humping. A tail came from somewhere under his armpit and wrapped quickly around my wrist.

Now, as a librarian in a children's department I have had my share of snake programs, and reptiles as such do not frighten me. Spiders I am not so sanguine about. But snakes are not a phobia of mine. Except for a quick intake of breath, brought on by surprise, not fear, I did not loose my grip.

The old man gave a *humph*, a grudging sound of approval, closed his eyes, and roared like a lion. I have seen movies. I have watched documentaries. I know the difference. All of Africa was in that sound.

I laughed. "All right, whoever you are, enough games," I said. "What's going on?"

He sat up slowly, opened those clean blue eyes, and said, "Wrong question, my dear." He had a slight accent I could not identify. "You are supposed to ask, 'What *will* go on?' "

Angrily, I let go of his shoulder. "Obviously you need no help. I'm leaving."

"Yes," he said. "I know." Then, incredibly, he turned over on his side. A partial stuttering snore began at once. Then a whiff of that voice came at me again. "But of course you *will* be back."

"Of course I *will* not!" I said huffily. As an exit line it lacked both dignity and punch, but it was all I could manage as I walked off. Before I had reached the big rock, the seals had settled down around him again. I know because they were singing their lullabies over the roar of his snore—and I peeked. The smell followed me most of the way back home.

Once back in the lighthouse, a peculiar lethargy claimed me. I seemed to know something I did not want to know. A story suddenly recalled. I deliberately tried to think of everything but the old man. I stared out the great windows, a sight that always delighted me. Sky greeted me, a pallid slate of sky written on by guillemots and punctuated by gulls. A phalanx of herring gulls sailed by followed by a pale ghostly shadow that I guessed might be an Iceland gull. Then nothing but sky. I don't believe I even blinked.

The phone shrilled.

I picked it up and could not even manage a hello until Mike's voice recalled me to time and place.

"Aunt Lyssa. Are you there? Are you all right? I tried to call before and there was no answer."

I snapped myself into focus. "Yes, Mike. I'm fine. Tell me a story."

There was a moment of crackling silence at the other end. Then a throat clearing. "A story? Say, are you sure you're all right?"

"I'm sure."

"Well, what do you mean—a story?"

I held on to the phone with both hands as if to coax his answer. As if I had foresight. I knew his answer already. "About an old man, with seals," I said.

Silence.

"You're the classics scholar, Mike. Tell me about Proteus."

"Try Bulfinch." He said it for a laugh. He had long ago taught me that Bulfinch was not to be trusted, for he had allowed no one to edit him, had made mistakes. "Why do you need to know?"

"A poem," I said. "A reference." No answer, but answer enough.

The phone waited a heartbeat, then spoke in Mike's voice. "One old man, with seals, coming up. One smelly old god, with seals, Aunt Lyssa. He was a shape-changer with the ability to foretell the future, only you had to hold on to him through all his changes to make him talk. Ulysses was able . . ."

"I remember," I said. "I know."

I hung up. The old man had been right. Of course I would be back. In the morning.

In the morning I gathered up pad, pencils, a sweater, and the flask of Earl Grey tea I had prepared. I stuffed them all into my old backpack. Then I started out as soon as light had

74

bleached a line across the rocks.

Overhead a pair of Laughing gulls wrote along the wind's pages with their white-bordered wings. I could almost read their messages, so clear and forceful was the scripting. Even the rocks signed to me, the water murmured advice. It was as if the world was a storyteller, a singer of old songs. The seas along the coast, usually green-black, seemed wine-dark and full of a churning energy. I did not need to hurry. I knew he would be there. Sometimes foresight has as much to do with reason as with magic.

The whale rock signaled me, and the smell lured me on. When I saw the one, and the other found my nose, I smiled. I made the last turning, and there he was—asleep and snoring.

I climbed down carefully and watched the seals scatter before me, then I knelt by his side.

I shook my head. Here was the world's oldest, dirtiest, smelliest man. A bum vomited up by the ocean. The centuries layered on his skin. And here was I thinking he was a god.

Then I shrugged and reached out to grab his shoulder. Fire. Water. Snake. Lion. I would outwait them all.

Of course I knew the question I would *not* ask. No one my age needs to know the exact time of dying. But the other questions, the ones that deal with the days and months and years after I would surely be gone, I would ask them all. And he,

being a god who cannot lie about the future, must tell me everything, everything that is going to happen in the world.

After all, I am a stubborn old woman. And a curious one.
And I have always had a passion for the news.

Davy Jones' Locker

Davy Jones has a sand bar
that is under water twice a day.
There he serves liquid refreshment
to passing mermen,
which is why, I suppose,
so many of the merrow
sport red noses
and sing sea chanteys
at the top of their voices
in the middle of the night.

The Fisherman's Wife

John Merton was a fisherman. He brought up eels and elvers, little finny creatures and great sharp-toothed monsters from the waves. He sold their meat at markets and made necklaces of their teeth for the fairs.

If you asked him, he would say that what he loved about the ocean was its vast silence, and wasn't that why he had married him a wife the same. Deaf she was, and mute too, but she could talk with her hands, a flowing syncopation. He would tell you that, and it would be no lie. But there were times when he would go mad with her silences, as the sea can drive men mad, and he would leave the house to seek the babble of the market-place. As meaningful as were her finger fantasies, they brought his ear no respite from the quiet.

There was one time, though, that he left too soon, and it happened this way. It was a cold and gray morning, and he slammed the door on his wife, thinking she would not know it, forgetting there are other ways to hear. And as he walked along the shore, singing loudly to himself—so as to prime his ears— and swinging the basket of fish pies he had for the fair, he heard only the sound of his own voice. The hush of the waves might have told him something. The silence of the seabirds wheeling overhead.

"Buy my pies," he sang out in practice, his boots cutting great gashes like exclamation marks in the sand.

Then he saw something washed up on the beach ahead.

Now fishermen often find things left along the shore. The sea gives and it takes and as often gives back again. There is sometimes a profit to be turned on the gifts of the sea. But every fisherman knows that when you have dealings with the deep you leave something of yourself behind.

It was no flotsam lying on the sand. It was a sea-queen, beached and gasping. John Merton stood over her, and his feet were as large as her head. Her body had a pale-greenish cast to it. The scales of her fishlike tail ran up past her waist, and some small scales lay along her sides, sprinkled like shiny gray-green freckles on the paler skin. Her breasts were as smooth and golden as shells. Her supple shoulders and arms looked almost boneless. The green-brown hair that flowed from her head was the color and texture of wrackweed. There was nothing lovely about her at all, he thought, though she exerted an alien fascination. She struggled for breath and, finding it, blew it out again in clusters of large, luminescent bubbles that made a sound as of waves against the shore.

And when John Merton bent down to look at her more closely still, it was as if he had dived into her eyes. They were ocean eyes, blue-green, and with golden flecks in the iris like minnows darting about. He could not stop staring. She seemed to call to him with those eyes, a calling louder than any sound could be in the air. He thought he heard his name, and yet he knew that she could not have spoken it. And he could not ask the mermaid about it, for how could she tell him? All fishermen know that mermaids cannot speak. They have no tongues.

He bent down and picked her up and her tail wrapped around his waist, quick as an eel. He unwound it slowly, reluctantly, from his body and then, with a convulsive shudder, threw her from him back into the sea. She flipped her tail once, sang out in a low ululation, and was gone.

He thought, wished really, that that would be the end of it, though he could not stop shuddering. He fancied he could still feel the tail around him, coldly constricting. He went on to the fair, sold all his pies, drank up the profit and started for home.

He tried to convince himself that he had seen stranger things in the water. Worse—and better. Hadn't he one day brought up a shark with a man's hand in its stomach? A right hand with a ring on the third finger, a ring of tourmaline and gold that he now wore himself, vanity getting the better of superstition. He could have given it to his wife, Mair, but he kept it for himself, forgetting that the sea would have its due. And hadn't he one night seen the stars reflecting their cold brilliance on the water as if the ocean itself stared up at him with a thousand thousand eyes? Worse—and better. He reminded himself of his years culling the tides that swept rotting boards and babies' shoes and kitchen cups to his feet. And the fish. And the eels. And the necklaces of teeth. Worse—and better.

By the time he arrived home he had convinced himself of nothing but the fact that the mermaid was the nastiest and yet most compelling thing he had yet seen in the ocean. Still, he said nothing of it to Mair, for though she was a fisherman's daughter and a fisherman's wife, since she had been deaf from birth no one had ever let her go out to sea. He did not want her to be frightened; as frightened as he was himself.

But Mair learned something of it, for that night when John Merton lay in bed with the great down quilt over him, he swam and cried and swam again in his sleep, keeping up stroke for stroke with the sea-queen. And he called out, "Cold, oh God, she's so cold," and pushed Mair away when she tried to wrap her arms around his waist for comfort. Oh, yes, she knew, even though she could not hear him, but what could she do? If he would not listen to her hands on his, there was no more help she could give.

So John Merton went out the next day with only his wife's silent prayer picked out by her fingers along his back. He did not turn for a kiss.

And when he was out no more than half a mile, pulling strongly on the oars and ignoring the spray, the sea-queen leaped like a shot across his bow. He tried to look away, but he was not surprised. He tried not to see her webbed hand on the oarlock or the fingers as sure as wrackweed that gripped his wrist. But slowly, ever so slowly, he turned and stared at her, and the little golden fish in her eyes beckoned to him. Then he heard her speak, a great hollow of sound somewhere between a sigh and a song, that came from the grotto that was her mouth.

"I will come," he answered, now sure of her question, hearing in it all he had longed to hear from his wife. It was magic, to be sure, a compulsion, and he could not have denied it had he tried. He stood up, drew off his cap and tossed it onto the waves. Then he let the oars slip away and his life on land slip away and plunged into the water near the bobbing cap just a beat behind the mermaid's flashing tail.

A small wave swamped his boat. It half sank, and the tide

lugged it relentlessly back to the shore where it lay on the beach like a bloated whale.

When they found the boat, John Merton's mates thought him drowned. And they came to the house, their eyes tight with grief and their hands full of unsubtle mimings.

"He is gone," said their hands. "A husband to the sea." For they never spoke of death and the ocean in the same breath, but disguised it with words of celebration.

Mair thanked them with her fingers for the news they bore, but she was not sure that they told her the truth. Remembering her husband's night dreams, she was not sure at all. And as she was a solitary person by nature, she took her own counsel. Then she waited until sunrise and went down to the shore.

His boat was now hers by widow's right. Using a pair of borrowed oars, she wrestled it into the sea.

She had never been away from shore, and letting go of the land was not an easy thing. Her eyes lingered on the beach and sought out familiar rocks, a twisted tree, the humps of other boats that marked the shore. But at last she tired of the land-marks that had become so unfamiliar, and turned her sights to the sea.

Then, about half a mile out, where the sheltered bay gave way to the open sea, she saw something bobbing on the waves. A sodden blue knit cap. John Merton's marker.

"He sent it to me," Mair thought. And in her eagerness to have it, she almost loosed the oars. But she calmed herself and rowed to the cap, fishing it out with her hands. Then she shipped the oars and stood up. Tying a great strong rope around her waist, with one end knotted firmly through the oarlock—not a sailor's knot but a loveknot, the kind that she might have plaited in her hair—Mair flung herself at the ocean.

Down and down and down she went, through the seven layers of the sea.

At first it was warm, with a cool, light-blue color hung with crystal teardrops. Little spotted fish, green and gold, were caught in each drop. And when she touched them, the bubbles burst and freed the fish, which darted off and out of sight.

The next layer was cooler, an aquamarine with a fine, falling rain of gold. In and out of these golden strings swam slower creatures of the deep: bulging squid, ribboned sea snakes, knobby five-fingered stars. And the strands of gold parted before her like a curtain of beads and she could peer down into the colder, darker layers below.

Down and down and down Mair went until she reached the ocean floor at last. And there was a path laid out, of finely colored sands edged round with shells, and statues made of bone. Anemones on their fleshy stalks waved at her as she passed, for her passage among them was marked with the swirlings of a strange new tide.

At last she came to a palace that was carved out of coral. The doors and windows were arched and open, and through them passed the creatures of the sea.

Mair walked into a single great hall. Ahead of her, on a small dais, was a divan made of coral, pink and gleaming. On this coral couch lay the sea-queen. Her tail and hair moved to the sway of the currents, but she was otherwise quite still. In the shadowed, filtered light of the hall, she seemed ageless and very beautiful.

Mair moved closer, little bubbles breaking from her mouth like fragments of unspoken words. Her movement set up countercurrents in the hall. And suddenly, around the edges of her sight, she saw another movement. Turning, she saw ranged around her an army of bones, the husbands of the sea. Not a shred or tatter of skin clothed them, yet every skeleton was an armature from which the bones hung, as surely connected as they had been on land. The skeletons bowed to her, one after another, but Mair could see that they moved not on their own reckoning, but danced to the tunes piped through them by the tides. And though on land they would have each looked different, without hair, without eyes, without the subtle coverings of flesh, they were all the same.

Mair covered her eyes with her hands for a moment, then she

looked up. On the couch, the mermaid was smiling down at her with her tongueless mouth. She waved a supple arm at one whole wall of bone men and they moved again in the aftermath of her greeting.

"Please," said Mair, "please give me back my man." She spoke with her hands, the only pleadings she knew. And the tongueless sea-queen seemed to understand, seemed to sense a sisterhood between them and gave her back greetings with fingers that swam as swiftly as any little fish.

Then Mair knew that the mermaid was telling her to choose, choose one of the skeletons that had been men. Only they all looked alike, with their sea-filled eye sockets and their bony grins.

"I will try," she signed, and turned toward them.

Slowly she walked the line of bitter bones. The first had yellow minnows fleeting through its hollow eyes. The second had a twining of green vines round its ribs. The third laughed a school of red fish out its mouth. The fourth had a pulsing anemone heart. And so on down the line she went, thinking with quiet irony of the identity of flesh.

But as long as she looked, she could not tell John Merton from the rest. If he was there, he was only a hanging of bones, indistinguishable from the others.

She turned back to the divan to admit defeat, when a flash of green and gold caught her eye. It was a colder color than the rest—yet warmer, too. It was alien under the sea, as alien as she, and she turned toward its moving light.

And then, on the third finger of one skeleton's hand, she saw it—the tourmaline ring which her John had so prized. Pushing through the water toward him, sending dark eddies to the walls that set the skeletons writhing in response, she took up his skeletal hand. The fingers were brittle and stiff under hers.

Quickly she untied the rope at her waist and looped it around the bones. She pulled them across her back and the white remnants of his fingers tightened around her waist.

She tried to pull the ring from his hand, to leave something there for the sea. But the white knucklebones resisted. And though she feared it, Mair went hand over hand, hand over hand along the rope, and pulled them both out of the sea.

She never looked back. And yet if she had looked, would she have seen the sea replace her man layer by layer? First it stuck the tatters of flesh and blue-green rivulets of veins along the bones. Then it clothed muscle and sinew with a fine covering of skin. Then hair and nails and the decorations of line. By the time they had risen through the seven strata of the sea, he looked like John Merton once again.

But she, who had worked so hard to save him, could not swim, and so it was John Merton himself who untied the rope and got them back to the boat. And it was John Merton himself who pulled them aboard and rowed them both to shore.

And a time later, when Mair Merton sat up in bed ready at last to taste a bit of the broth he had cooked for her, she asked him in her own way what it was that had occurred.

"John Merton," she signed, touching his fine strong arms with their covering of tanned skin and fine golden hair. "Tell me . . ."

But he covered her hands with his, the hand that was still wearing the gold and tourmaline ring. He shook his head and the look in his eyes was enough. For she could suddenly see past the sea-green eyes to the sockets beneath, and she understood that although she had brought him home, a part of him would be left in the sea forever, for the sea takes its due.

He opened his mouth to her then, and she saw it was hollow, as dark black as the deeps, and filled with the sound of waves.

"Never mind, John Merton," she signed on his hand, on his arms around her, into his hair. "The heart can speak, though the mouth be still. I will be loving you all the same."

And, of course, she did.

The Mermaid
to Her Glass

Tiny golden minnows
swim in the green pools
of my eyes.
My skin is the color
of ocean foam.
Only where my tail begins
little green scales
cluster like cockleshells
tossed up on the sand.

My tail in repose
is a question mark
which I answer
with my smile.
Will he look at me?
Will he speak?
A pinch to my cheeks
for color,
for luck,
and the cowries
for my green-gold hair.
Great Lir,
let him ask me
for just one dance.

The River Maid

There was once a rich farmer named Jan who decided to expand his holdings. He longed for the green meadow that abutted his farm with a passion that amazed him. But a swift river ran between the two. It was far too wide and far too deep for his cows to cross.

He stood on the riverbank and watched the water hurtle over its rocky course.

"I could build a bridge," he said aloud. "But, then, any fool could do that. And I am no fool."

At his words the river growled, but Jan did not heed it.

"No!" Jan said with a laugh, "I shall build no bridge across this water. I shall make the river move aside for me." And so he planned how he would dam it up, digging a canal along the outer edge of the meadow, and thus allow his cows the fresh green grass.

As if guessing Jan's thought, the river roared out, tumbling stones in its rush to be heard. But Jan did not understand it. Instead, he left at once to go to the town where he purchased the land and supplies.

The men Jan hired dug and dug for weeks until a deep ditch and a large dam had been built. Then they watched as the river slowly filled up behind the dam. And when, at Jan's signal, the gate to the canal was opened, the river was forced to move into its new course and leave its comfortable old bed behind.

At that, Jan was triumphant. He laughed and turned to the waiting men. "See!" he called out loudly, "I am not just Jan the Farmer. I am Jan the River Tamer. A wave of my hand, and the water must change its way."

His words troubled the other men. They spat between their fingers and made other signs against the evil eye. But Jan paid them no mind. He was the last to leave the river's side that evening and went home well after dark.

The next morning Jan's feeling of triumph had not faded and he went down again to the path of the old river, which was now no more than mud and mire. He wanted to look at the desolation and dance over the newly dried stones.

But when he got to the river's old bed, he saw someone lying faceup in the center of the waterless course. It was a girl clothed only in a white shift that clung to her body like a skin.

Fearing her dead, Jan ran through the mud and knelt by her side. He put out his hand but could not touch her. He had never seen anyone so beautiful.

Fanned out about her head, her hair was a fleece of gold, each separate strand distinguishable. Fine gold hairs lay molded on her forearms and like wet down upon her legs. On each of her closed eyelids a drop of river water glistened and reflected back to him his own staring face.

At last Jan reached over and touched her cheek, and at his touch, her eyes opened wide. He nearly drowned in the blue of them.

He lifted the girl up in his arms, never noticing how cold her skin or how the mud stuck nowhere to her body or her shift, and he carried her up onto the bank. She gestured once toward the old riverbank and let out a single mewling cry. Then she curled in toward his body, nestling, and seemed to sleep.

Not daring to wake her again, Jan carried her home and put her down by the hearth. He lit the fire, though it was late spring and the house already quite warm. Then he sat by the sleeping girl and stared.

She lay in a curled position for some time. Only the slow

pulsing of her back told him that she breathed. But, as dusk settled about the house, bringing with it a half-light, the girl gave a sudden sigh and stretched. Then she sat up and stared. Her arms went out before her as if she were swimming in the air. Jan wondered for a moment if she were blind.

Then the girl leaped up in one fluid movement and began to sway, to dance upon the hearthstones. Her feet beat swiftly and she turned round and round in dizzying circles. She stopped so suddenly that Jan's head still spun. He saw that she was now perfectly dry except for one side of her shift; the left hem and skirt were still damp and remained molded against her.

"Turn again," Jan whispered hoarsely, suddenly afraid.

The girl looked at him and did not move.

When he saw that she did not understand his tongue, Jan walked over to her and led her back to the fire. Her hand was quite cold in his. But she smiled shyly up at him. She was small, only chest high, and Jan himself was not a large man. Her skin, even in the darkening house, was so white it glowed with a fierce light. Jan could see the rivulets of her veins where they ran close to the surface, at her wrists and temples.

He stayed with her by the fire until the heat made him sweat. But though she stood silently, letting the fire warm her first one side and then the other, her skin remained cold, and the left side of her shift would not dry.

Jan knelt down before her and touched the damp hem. He put his cheek against it.

"Huttah!" he cried at last. "I know you now. You are a river maid. A water spirit. I have heard of such. I believed in them when I was a child."

The water girl smiled steadily down at him and touched his hair with her fingers, twining the strands round and about as if weaving a spell.

Jan felt the touch, cold and hot, burn its way down the back of his head and along his spine. He remembered with dread all the old tales. To hold such a one against her will meant death. To love such a one meant despair.

He shook his head violently and her hand fell away. "How foolish," Jan thought. "Old wives and children believe such things. I do not love her, beautiful as she is. And as for the other, how am I to know what is her will? If we cannot talk the same tongue, I can only guess her wants." He rose and went to the cupboard and took out bread and cheese and a bit of salt fish which he put before her.

The water maid ate nothing. Not then or later. She had only a few drops of water before the night settled in.

When the moon rose, the river maid began to pace restlessly about the house. From one wall to the other, she walked. She went to the window and put her hand against the glass. She stood by the closed door and put her shoulder to the wood, but she would not touch the metal latch.

It was then that Jan was sure of her. "Cold iron will keep her in." He was determined she would stay at least until morning.

The river maid cried all the night, a high keening that rose and fell like waves. But in the morning she seemed accommodated to the house and settled quietly to sleep by the fire. Once in a while, she would stretch and stand, the damp left side of her shift clinging to her thigh. In the half-light of the hearth she seemed even more beautiful than before.

Jan left a bowl of fresh water near the fire, with some cress by it, before he went to feed the cows. But he checked the latch on the windows and set a heavy iron bar across the outside of the door.

"I will let you go tonight," he promised slowly. "*Tonight*," he said, as if speaking to a child. But she did not know his language and could not hold him to his vow.

By the next morning, he had forgotten making it.

For a year Jan kept her. He grew to like the wavering sounds she made as she cried each night. He loved the way her eyes turned a deep green when he touched her. He was fascinated by the blue veins that meandered at her throat, along the backs of her knees, and laced each small breast. Her mouth was always cold under his.

Fearing the girl might guess the working of window or gate, Jan fashioned iron chains for the glass and an ornate grillwork for the door. In that way, he could open them to let in air and let her look out at the sun and moon and season's changes. But he did not let her go. And as she never learned to speak with him in his tongue and thereby beg for release, Jan convinced himself that she was content.

Then it was spring again. Down from the mountains came the swollen streams, made big with melted snow. The river maid drank whole glasses of water now, and put on weight. Jan guessed that she carried his child, for her belly grew, she moved slowly and no longer tried to dance. She sat by the window at night with her arms raised and sang strange, wordless tunes, sometimes loud and sometimes soft as a cradle song. Her voice was as steady as the patter of the rain, and underneath Jan fancied he heard a growing strength. His nights became as restless as hers, his sleep full of watery dreams.

The night of the full moon, the rain beat angrily against the glass as if insisting on admission. The river maid put her head to one side, listening. Then she rose and left her window place. She stretched and put her hands to her back, then traced them slowly around her sides to the front. She moved heavily to the hearth and sat. Bracing both hands on the stones behind her, she spread her legs, crooked at the knees.

Jan watched as her belly rolled in great waves under the tight white shift.

She threw her head back, gasped at the air, and then, with a great cry of triumph, expelled the child. It rode a gush of water between her legs and came to rest at Jan's feet. It was small and fishlike, with a translucent tail. It looked up at him with blue eyes that were covered with a veil of skin. The skin lifted once, twice, then closed again as the child slept.

Jan cried because it was a beast.

At that very moment, the river outside gave a shout of release. With the added waters from the rain and snow, it had the strength to push through the earth dam. In a single wave, that gathered force as it rolled, it rushed across the meadow, through the farmyard and barn, and overwhelmed the house. It broke the iron gates and grilles as if they were brittle sticks, washing them away in its flood. Then it settled back into its old course, tumbling over familiar rocks and rounding the curves it had cut in its youth.

When the neighbors came the next day to assess the damage, they found no trace of the house or of Jan.

"Gone," said one.

"A bad end," said another.

"Never change a river," said a third.

They spat through their fingers and made other signs against evil. Then they went home to their own fires and gave it no more thought.

But a year later, in a pocket of the river, in a quiet place said to house a great fish with a translucent tail, an inquisitive boy found a jumble of white bones.

His father and the other men guessed the bones to be Jan's, and they left them to the river instead of burying them.

When the boy asked why, his father said, "Huttah! Hush, boy, and listen."

The boy listened and heard the river playing merrily over the bones. It was a high, sweet, bubbling song. And anyone with half an ear could hear that the song, though wordless, or at least in a language unknown to men, was full of freedom and a conquering joy.

The Merman in Love

Overhead a boat sails by,
the ripples in its wake
as quick and white
as the underwings of a gull.
Somewhere the sperm whale sings
his lonely lowings
along the current.
I am not deaf,
do not think I am deaf
to the music he makes.

But the songs
her fingers croon
and the bubbled melodies
from her mouth
are more beautiful to me
than whale songs,
than the solo notes of gulls
skimming low over the waves,
than the mournful mating call
of the foghorn
as it cries its love
to the sea.

The Corridors of the Sea

"He's awfully small for a hero," said the green-smocked technician. He smirked as the door irised closed behind the object of his derision.

"The better to sneak through the corridors of the sea," answered his companion, a badge-two doctoral candidate. Her voice implied italics.

"Well, Eddystone *is* a kind of hero," said a third, coming up behind them suddenly and leaning uninvited into the conversation. "He invented the Breather. Why shouldn't he be the one to try it out? There's only one Breather, after all."

"And only one Eddystone," the woman said, a shade too quickly. "And wouldn't you know he'd make the Breather too small for anyone but himself."

"Still, he *is* the one who's risking his life."

"Don't *cousteau* us, Gabe Whitcomb." The tech was furious. "There aren't supposed to be any heroes on Hydrospace. We do this together or we don't do it at all. It's thinking like that that almost cost us our funding last year."

Whitcomb had no answer to the charge, parroted as it was from the very releases he wrote for the telereports and interlab memos, words he believed in.

The three separated and Whitcomb headed through the door after Eddystone. The other two went down the lift to their own lab section. They were not involved with the Breather test, whose techs wore yellow smocks. Rather, they were working on developing the elusive fluid-damping skin.

"Damned jealous Dampers," Whitcomb whispered to himself as he stepped through the door. But at the moment of speaking, he knew his anger was useless and, in fact, wrong. The Dampers of the lab *might* indeed be jealous that the Breather project had developed faster and come to fruition first. But it should not matter in as compact a group as Hydrospace IV. What affected one, affected all. That was canon here. That was why hero-worship was anathema to them. All except Tom Eddystone, little Tommy Eddystone, who went his own inimitable way and answered his own siren song. He hadn't changed, Gabe mused, in the thirty years they had been friends.

106

Eddystone was ahead of him, in his bathing suit and tank top, moving slowly down the hall. It was easy for Gabe to catch up. Not only were Eddystone's strides shorter than most, but the recent Breather operation gave him a gingerly gait, as if he had an advanced case of Parkinson's. He walked on the balls of his feet, leaning forward. He carried himself carefully now, compensating for the added weight of the Breather organs.

"Tommy," Gabe called out breathlessly, pretending he had to hurry and wanted Eddystone to wait. It was part of a built-in tact that made him such an excellent tele-flak. But Eddystone was not fooled. It was just a game they always played.

Eddystone stopped and turned slowly, moving as if he were going through water. Or mud. Gabe wondered at the strain that showed in his eyes. Probably the result of worry, since the doctors all agreed that the time for pain from the operation itself should be past.

"Are you ready for the press conference?" Gabe's question was *pro forma*. Eddystone was always ready to promote his ideas. He was a man who lived comfortably in his head and always invited others to come in for a visit.

A scowl was Eddystone's answer.

For a moment Gabe wondered if the operation had affected Eddystone's personality as well. Then he shrugged and cuffed the little man lightly on the shoulder. "Come on, Tom-the-giant-killer," he said, a name he had invented for Eddystone when they had been in grade school together and Tommy's tongue had more than once gotten them both out of scrapes.

Eddystone smiled a bit and the triple striations under his collarbones, the most visible reminders of the operation, reddened. Then he opened and shut his mouth several times like a fish out of water, gasping for breath.

"Tommy, are you all right?" Gabe's concern was evident in every word.

"I've just been Down Under is all," Eddystone said in his high, reedy voice.

"And . . ." Gabe prompted.

Eddystone's mouth got thin. "And . . . it's easier Down Under." He suddenly looked right up into Gabe's eyes and reached for his friend's arms. His grip was stronger than those fine bones would suggest. Eddystone worked out secretly with weights. Only Gabe knew about it. "And it's becoming harder and harder each time to come back to shore."

"Harder?" The question hung between them, but Eddystone did not elaborate. He turned away slowly and once more moved gingerly down the hall toward the press room. He did not speak again and Gabe walked equally silent beside him.

Once in the room, Eddystone went right to the front and slumped into the armchair that sat before the charts and screen.

He paid no attention to the reporters and Hydrospace aides who clustered around him.

Gabe stopped to shake hands with reporters and camera persons he recognized, and he recognized most of them. That was his job, after all, and he was damned good at it. For the moment he managed to take their attention away from Eddystone, who was breathing heavily. But by the time Gabe had organized everyone into chairs, Eddystone had recovered and was sitting, quietly composed and waiting.

"Ladies and gentlemen," Gabe began, then gave a big smile. "Or rather I should say, *friends,* since we have all been through a lot together at Hydrospace IV." He waited for the return smiles, got them, and continued. "Most of you already know about our attempts here at the labs." He gestured to include the aides in his remarks.

"And I know that some of you have made some pretty shrewd guesses as to Dr. Eddystone's recent disappearance. In fact, one of you . . ." and he turned to speak directly to Janney Hyatt, the dark-haired science editor of the ERA channels, " . . . even ferreted out his hospital stay. But none of you came close to the real news. So we are going to give it to you straight. Today."

The reporters buzzed and the camera operators jockeyed for position.

"As you can see, Dr. Eddystone is not in his usual three-piece suit." Gabe turned and nodded at the chair. It drew an appreciative chuckle because Eddystone rarely dressed up, jeans and a dirty sweatshirt being his usual costume. He never tried to impress anyone with his physical appearance since he knew it was so unprepossessing. He was less than five feet tall, large nosed, popeyed. But his quick mind, his brilliant yet romantic scientific insights, his ability to make even the dullest listener understand the beauty he perceived in science, made his sweatshirt a uniform, the dirt stains badges.

"In fact, Dr. Eddystone is wearing his swim suit plus a tank top so as not to offend the sensibilities of any watchers out there in newsland."

Some of the reporters applauded at this, but Janney Hyatt scowled. Even the suggestion of sensibilities filled her with righteous indignation, as if Gabe had suggested it was women's sensibilities he was referring to.

"Dr. Eddystone has been *Down Under,* our designation of the water world around Hydrospace IV. It is his third trip this week and he wore just what you see him in now, minus the tank top, of course. He was under for twenty minutes the first time. The second time he stayed under forty minutes. And this last time— Dr. Eddystone?"

Eddystone held his reply until every eye was on him. Then he spoke, his light voice carrying to the back of the room. "I was under sixty minutes. I breathe harder on land now than I do in the sea."

There was bedlam in the room as the reporters jumped up, trying to ask questions. Finally one question shouted above the others spoke for them all. "You mean you were under sixty minutes *without* scuba gear?"

"Without anything," said Eddystone, standing up for effect. "As you see me."

The silence that followed was palpable and Gabe walked into it with his prepared speech. "You know that living under water has always been the goal of this particular Hydrospace lab: living under water *without* mechanical apparatus or bubble cities." It was a slight dig at the Hydrospace labs I, II, and III, and he hoped he would be forgiven it in the flush of their success. "That is what all our experiments, as secret as they have had to be, are all about. Dr. Eddystone headed the project on what we have called the Breather. Dr. Lemar's group has been working on a fluid-damping skin."

Everyone was listening. A few were taking notes. The cameras rolled. Gabe could feel the attention, and continued.

"When we first decided to prepare the bionics to allow a person to breathe water as easily as air, we took a lot of ribbing. Conservative marine biologists dubbed our lab *Eddystone's Folly* and our group the *Cousteau Corporation*. But we knew that the science was there. We had two possible approaches we were considering.

"The first was to implant a mechanical system which would extract the dissolved oxygen from the water and present it directly to the lungs. From there on, normal physiology would take over. The other choice was to implant a biological system, such as gills, from some chosen fish, which would load the blood directly with oxygen, thus bypassing the lungs."

Eddystone sat quietly, nodding at each point Gabe ticked off. Gabe looked around the room for questions. There were none.

"Of course you realize," he continued, "that both systems required the normal functioning of the musculature of breathing: one to pull the oxygen from the apparatus, the other to pass water over the implanted gills."

Janney Hyatt raised her hand and, to soothe her earlier anger at his "sensibilities" remark, Gabe called on her at once.

"What was the mechanical system to be made of?" she asked.

"Good question," said Gabe. "The earlier bionics experts felt more comfortable with metal, plastics, and electronics. So they opted for a dioxygenation module, *Doxymod*, which was basically an add-on option for the underwater human. We were going to try it on some dogs first, water dogs, possibly Labradors or a springer spaniel. Trouble surfaced immediately."

Laughter stopped Gabe until he realized his unintentional pun. He smiled and shrugged winningly and went on. "Making a *Doxymod* small enough and light enough was the first problem, of course. And once we had produced it—Dr. Eddystone and his staff produced it—we could think of no good reason to implant it. It needed batteries and that meant it had a built-in time limit. Just what we had been trying to avoid. All we had, after all that work, was tankless scuba gear. We were simply replacing the oxygen tanks with batteries. More mobile, perhaps, but . . ."

"In other words," added one of Eddystone's aides brightly, "not a fail-safe system. Batteries run down and need recharging."

The reporters whispered together. One tentatively raised his hand, but Gabe ignored him. He felt things building and, like any good performer, he knew it was time to continue.

"So we turned to the gill system. Modern medicine had already solved the rejection syndrome, as you know, at least *within* phylum. Using pigs for heart valves and the like. But we knew nothing about cross-phyla work. We expected a lot of trouble—and were surprised when we encountered very little. Men and fish, it turns out, go well together. Something seafood lovers have long been aware of! In fact, it occurred to one of our bright-eyed tech threes on a dissertation project that we could even produce a classically composed mermaid with a small woman and a large grouper tail. Could—if anyone could think of good reason why, that is."

It drew the laugh Gabe expected. Even Janney Hyatt smiled quickly before reverting to her customary scowl.

Gabe nodded once to his assistant sitting in the far back next to the projector. She caught his signal and dimmed the lights, flicking on the projector at the same time. The first slide focused automatically above Eddystone's head. It was of a large tuna on a white background, with five smaller fish below it. Gabe took up the pointer which had been resting against the table and placed the tip on the big fish.

"A lot of time and thought went into the question of whether to use the gills of a human-sized fish like this tuna or an array of smaller gills taken from several fish, perhaps even from different species." He pointed in turn to the other fish on the screen, naming them. "But as often happens in science, the simple solution proved best. Two large gills were inserted in the skin, just under the collar bones. . . ." The next slide, a detailed sketch of a human figure, appeared. "And ducts leading from the branchial passages through triune openings completed the alterations."

The next slides, in rapid succession, were of the actual operation.

"Valves were implanted, special plastic valves, that allowed either the lungs or the gills to be used. These went into the throat."

"So you made an amphibian," called out a gray-haired science writer from the *Times*.

"That was our intention," said Eddystone, standing up slowly. The final slide, of fish in the ocean, had snicked into place and was now projected onto his body. He threw an enormous shadow onto the screen.

Sensing an Eddystone speech, Gabe signaled his assistant with his hand, but she was already ahead of him, flicking off the projector and raising the lights.

"But something more happened. Think of it," said Eddystone. "We can walk on the moon, but not live there. We cannot even attempt a landing on Venus or breathe the Martian air. But the waters of our own world are waiting for us. They cradled us when we took our first hesitant steps into higher phyla. Why even now, in the womb, the fetus floats in *la mer*, the mother sea. Our blood is liquid, our bodies mostly water. We speak of humankind's exodus from the sea as an improvement on the race. But I tell you now that our return to it will be even more momentous. I am not an explorer . . . not an explorer taking one giant step for mankind. I am a child going home some million years after leaving."

The speech seemed to have exhausted him. Eddystone slumped back into his chair. Gabe stood over him protectively. But his own thoughts warred with his emotions. Even for Eddystone it was a romantic, emotional outburst. A regular *cousteau*. Gabe knew that he had always been the more conservative of the two of them, but he worried anew that the Breather mechanism might be affecting Eddystone in ways that had not been calculated. He put a hand on his friend's shoulder and was appalled to find it slippery with sweat. Perhaps a fever had set in.

"That's all now, ladies and gentlemen," Gabe said smoothly to the audience, not letting his alarm show. "Tomorrow, tide and time willing, at 0900 hours, we will give you a demonstration of the Breather. Right now Dr. Eddystone has to be run through some last-minute lab tests. However, my assistants will see to it that you receive the information you need for the technical end of your reports. Each pack has scientific and historical details, charts, and a bio sheet on Dr. Eddystone, plus photos from the operation. Thank you for coming."

The reporters dutifully collected their material from the aides and tried to bully further answers from the staff while Gabe shepherded Eddystone out the door marked NO EN-

TRY/TECH ONLY. It locked behind him and would only respond to a code that Hydrospace workers knew.

In the deserted back hall, Eddystone turned. "What last-minute tests?" he asked.

"No tests," Gabe said. "Questions. And I want to do the asking. You are going to give me some straight answers, Tommy. No romances. No *cousteaus*. What's going on? I felt your shoulder in there. It's all sweaty. Are you running a fever? Is there rejection starting?"

Eddystone looked up at him and smiled. "Not rejection," he said, chuckling a bit at a projected joke. "Rather call it an acceptance."

"Make sense, Tommy. I'm a friend, remember. Your oldest friend." Gabe put out his hand as a gesture of goodwill and was surprised when Eddystone grabbed his hand, for his palm was slick.

Eddystone took Gabe's hand and ran it up and down his arm, across his chest where it was exposed. The gill slits were closed but the tissue was ridged and slightly puckered. Gabe wanted to flinch, controlled it.

"Feel this so-called sweat," Eddystone said. "You can't really see it, but it's there. I thought at first I was imagining it, but now I know. You feel it, too, Gabe. It's not sweat at all."

Gabe drew his hand away gently. "Then what the hell is it?"

"It's the body's way of accepting its new life—under water. It's the fluid-damping skin that Lemar and her kids have been trying for all these months. Seems you can't *build it in*, Gabe. But once the body has been readapted for life in the sea, *it just comes.*"

"Then we'd better test you out, Tommy. The lab is where you belong now." Gabe started walking.

"No, don't you see," Eddystone said to Gabe's back, "that's *not* where I belong. I belong in the sea." His voice was almost a whisper, but the passion in his statement was unmistakable.

"Lab first, Tommy. Or there won't be any 0900 for you—or any of us—tomorrow." Gabe continued to walk, and was relieved to hear Eddystone's footsteps following him. He had surprised himself with the firmness of his tone. After all, Eddystone was the head of the lab while he, Gabe, was only the link with outside, with the grants and the news. Yet Eddystone was letting himself be led, pushed, carried in a way he had never allowed before. As if he had lost his willpower, Gabe thought, and the thought bothered him.

They came into the lab and Gabe turned at last. Eddystone was as pale as fishbelly and starting to gasp again. There was no sign of that strange sweat on his body, yet when Gabe took his arm to lead him through the door, he could feel the moisture. The skin itself seemed to be impregnated with the invisible fluid.

The lab was typical of Hydrospace, being half aquarium. It had small enclosed tanks filled with fish and sea life as well as a single wall of glass fronting directly on the ocean. Since the lab was on the lowest Hydrospace floor, resting on ocean bottom, the window let the scientists keep an eye on the fish and plants within the ecosystem without the necessity of diving. For longer, far-ranging expeditions, there were several lab-subs and for divers working within a mile radius of Hydrospace, a series of locks and wet-rooms leading off the lab. There was no chance of the bends if a diver came and went from the bottom floor of Hydrospace IV.

Only two techs were in the lab, both in their identifying yellow smocks. One was feeding tank specimens, the other checking out the data on the latest mari-culture fields. They looked up, nodded briefly, and went back to work.

"Look," Eddystone said to Gabe in a lowered voice, "I'm going to go out there now and I want you to watch through the window. I'll stay close enough for you to track me. Tell me what happens out there. What *you* see. I know what *I* see. But it's like this skin. I need to know someone else sees it, too. When I come back in, you can make tests all night long if you want to. But

119

you have to see what happens to me Down Under."

Gabe shook his head. "I don't like it, Tommy. Let me get some of the techs. Lemar, too."

Eddystone smiled that crooked grin that turned his homely face into an irrepressible imp's countenance. "Just us, Gabe. The two of us. It's always been that way. I want you to see it first."

Gabe shook his head again, but reluctantly agreed. "If you promise to test. . . ."

"I promise you anything you want," Eddystone answered, a shade too quickly.

"Don't con me, Tommy. I know you too well. Have known you too long. You are the one person who isn't expendable on this project."

"I don't plan to be expended," Eddystone answered, grinning. He walked to the door that led to the series of locks, turned, and waved. "And give those techs," he said, signaling with his head, "give 'em the night off." Then he was gone through the door.

Gabe could hear the sounds of the pressure-changing device, clicking and sighing, through the intercom. He went over to the techs. "Dr. Eddystone wants me to clear the lab for a few hours."

"We were just leaving anyway," said one. To prove she was

finished, she reached up and pulled out a large barrette that had held her hair back in a tight bun. As the blondish hair spilled over her shoulders, she gave Gabe a quick noncommittal smile and shrugged out of the yellow smock. She folded it into a small, neat square and stowed it away in a locker. Her friend was a step behind. Once they had left the lab, Gabe turned on the red neon testing sign over the door and locked it. No one would be able to come in now.

He went to the window and waited. It took ten minutes for anyone to go through the entire series of locks into the water, over a half-hour for the same person to return. The locks could not be overridden manually, though there was a secret code for emergencies kept in a black book in Eddystone's file cabinet. He adjusted the special sea-specs that allowed him to see clearly through pressure-sensitive glass.

Right outside the station grew a hodgepodge of undersea plants. Some had been set in purposefully to act as hiding places for the smaller fish, to entice them closer to the window for easy viewing. Others had drifted in and attached themselves to the sides of the station, to the rock ledges left by the original builders of Hydrospace, to the sandy bottom of the sea.

While Gabe watched, a school of pout swam by, suddenly diving and turning together, on some kind of invisible signal. Though he knew the technical explanations for schooling—that the movement as a unit was made possible by visual stimulation and by pressure-sensitive lateral lines on each fish responding to the minutest vibrations in the water, the natural choreography of schooled fish never ceased to delight him. It was the one *cousteau* he permitted himself—that the fish danced. He was smiling when the school suddenly broke apart and re-formed far off to the right of the window, almost out of sight. A dark shadow was emerging from the locks. Eddystone.

Gabe had expected him to swim in the rolling overhand most divers affected. But, instead, Eddystone moved with the boneless insinuations of an eel. He seemed to undulate through the water, his feet and legs moving together, fluidly pumping him along. His arms were not overhead but by his side, the hands fluttering like fins. It was not a motion that a man should be able to make comfortably, yet he made it with a flowing ease that quickly brought him alongside the window. He turned once to stand upright so that Gabe could get a close look at him. With a shock, Gabe realized that Eddystone was entirely naked. He had not noticed it at first because Eddystone's genitals were not visible, as if they had retracted into the body cavity. Gabe moved closer and bumped his head against the glass.

As if the noise frightened him, Eddystone jerked back.

"Tommy!" Gabe cried out, a howl he did not at first recognize as his own. But the glass was too thick for him to be heard.

122

He tried to sign in the shorthand they had developed for divers, but before he could lift a finger, Eddystone had turned, pumped once, and was gone.

The second eyelid lifted and Eddystone stared at the world around him. The softly filtered light encouraged dreaming. He saw, on the periphery of clear sight, the flickerings of darting fish. Some subtle emanation floated on the stream past him. He flipped over, righted himself with a casual cupping of his palms and waited. He was not sure for what.

She came toward him trailing a line of lovers, but he saw only Her. The swirls of sea-green hair streamed behind Her, and there were tiny conch caught up like barrettes behind each ear. Her body was childlike, with underdeveloped breasts as perfect and pink as bubbleshells, and a tail that resembled legs, so deep was the cleft in it. When She stopped to look at him, Her hair swirled about Her body, masking Her breasts. Her eyes were as green as Her hair, Her mouth full and the teeth as small and white and rounded as pearls. She held a hand out to him, and the webbing between Her fingers was translucent and pulsing.

Eddystone moved toward Her, pulled on by a desire he could not name. But there were suddenly others there before him, four large, bullish-looking males with broad shoulders and deep chests and squinty little eyes. They ringed around Her, and one, more forward than the rest, put his hands on Her body and rubbed them up and down Her sides. She smiled and let the male touch Her for a moment, then pushed him away. He went back to the outer circle with the others, waiting. She held up Her hands again to Eddystone and he swam cautiously to Her touch.

Her skin was as smooth and fluid as an eel's, and his hands slipped easily up and over Her breasts. But he was bothered by the presence of the others and hesitated.

She flipped Her tail and was away, the line of males behind Her. They moved too quickly for him, and when they left, it was as if a spell were broken. He turned back toward the station.

"Tommy," Gabe's voice boomed into the locks. "I hear you in there. Where did you go? One minute you were here, then you took off after a herd of *Sirenia* and were gone."

The only answer from the intercom was a slow, stumbling hiss. Gabe could only guess that it was Eddystone's breathing readjusting to the air, as the implanted valves responded to the situation. But he did not like the sound, did not like it at all. When the last lock sighed open, he ran into it and found Eddystone collapsed on the floor, still naked and gasping.

"Tommy, wake up! For God's sake, get up." He knelt by Eddystone's side and ran his hands under his friend's neck. The slipperiness was more apparent than before. Picking him up, Gabe had to cradle Eddystone close against his chest to keep him from sliding away. As Gabe watched, the gill slits fluttered open and shut under Eddystone's collarbone.

"I've got to get you to MedCentral," he whispered into Eddystone's ear. "Something is malfunctioning with the valves. Hold on, buddy. I'll get you through." He ran through the lab and was working frantically to unlock the door without dropping Eddystone when he looked down. To his horror, Eddystone had halfway opened his eyes and one of them was partially covered with a second, transparent eyelid.

"Take me . . . take me back," Eddystone whispered.

"Not on your life," Gabe answered.

"It *is* on my life," Eddystone said in a hoarse, croaking voice.

Gabe stopped. "Tommy."

The membranous eyelid flicked open and he struggled in Gabe's arms. "It calls me," he said. "She calls."

"Tommy, I don't know what you mean—she. The sea? I don't even know what you *are*, anymore."

"I am what we were all meant to be, Gabe. Take me back. I can't breathe." His gasping, wheezing attempts at talking had already confirmed that.

Gabe turned around. "If I put you down, could you walk?"

"I don't know. Air strangling me."

"Then I'll carry you."

Eddystone grinned up at him, a grin as familiar as it was strange. "Good. I carried you long enough."

Gabe tried to laugh but couldn't. When they reached the locks, Gabe kicked the door open with his foot. "You're slippery as hell, you know," he said. He needed to say something.

"The better to sneak through the corridors of the sea," said Eddystone.

"God, Tommy, don't *cousteau* me now."

Eddystone shook his head slowly. "But he was right, you know, Jacques Cousteau. The poetry, the romance, the beauty, the longing for the secret other. Someone sang, 'What we lose on the land we will find in the sea.' It's all out there."

"Fish are out there, Tommy. And reefs. And the possibility of vast farms to feed a starving humanity. And sharks. And pods of whale. The mermaid is nothing more than a bad case of horniness or a near-sighted sailor looking at a manatee. Sea creatures don't build, Tommy. There are no houses and no factories under the water. Dolphin don't weave. Dugongs don't tell stories. And whale songs are only music because romantics believe them so. Come on, Tommy. You're a scientist. You know that. Metaphors are words. Words. They don't exist. They don't live."

Eddystone gave him that strange grin once more and threw out an old punch line at him. "You call *this* living?" He tried to laugh but began to wheeze instead.

Gabe hit at the lock mechanism with his elbow, and the door shut behind them. "I'm going Down Under with you this time, Tommy," he said.

"Yes and no," Eddystone answered cryptically.

Eddystone lay on the bench and watched as Gabe picked out one of the fits-all trunks from a hook. He slipped out of his clothes and got into the swimsuit, placing his clothes neatly on a hanger. When the timer announced the opening of the next lock, he was ready. He picked Eddystone up and walked through into the second room.

Depositing the little man on another bench, Gabe got into the scuba gear. There were always at least six tanks in readiness.

"Remember the first time we learned to dive?" Gabe asked. "And you were so excited, you didn't come off the bottom of the swimming pool until your air just about ran out and the instructor had fits?"

"I don't . . . don't remember," Eddystone said quietly in a very distant way.

"Of course you remember, Tommy."

Eddystone did not answer.

They went into the next room, Eddystone leaning heavily on

127

Gabe's arm. This was the first of the two wet-rooms, where the water fed slowly in through piping, giving divers time for any last-minute checks of their gear.

No sooner had the water started in than Eddystone rolled off the bench on which he had been lying and stretched out on the floor. The rising water puddled around him, slowly covering his body. As it closed over the gill slits in his chest, he smiled. It was the slow Eddystone smile that Gabe knew so well. Eddystone ran a finger in and around the gill slits as if cleaning them.

Gabe said nothing but watched as if he were discovering a new species.

When the door opened automatically, mixing the water in the first wet-room with the ocean water funneled into the second, Eddystone swam in alone. He swam under water, but Gabe walked along, keeping his head in the few inches of air. In the last lock, Eddystone surfaced for a moment and held a hand out toward Gabe. There was a strange webbing between the thumb and first finger that Gabe could swear had never been there before. Blue veins, as meandering as old rivers, ran through the webbing.

Gabe took the offered hand and held it up to his cheek. Without meaning to, he began to cry. Eddystone freed his hand and touched one of the tears.

"Salt," he whispered. "As salty as the sea. We are closer than

128

you think. Closer than you now accept."

Gabe bit down on his mouthpiece and sucked in the air. The last door opened and the sea flooded the rest of the chamber.

Eddystone was through the door in an instant. Even with flippers, Gabe was left far behind. He could only follow the faint trail of bubbles that Eddystone laid down. A trail that was dissipated in moments. There was nothing ahead of him but the vast ocean shot through with rays of filtered light. He kept up his search for almost an hour, then turned back alone.

He quartered the ocean bottom, searching for Her scent. Each minute under washed away memory, till he swam free of ambition and only instinct drove him on.

At last he slipped, by accident, into a current that brought him news of Her. The water, touching the fine hairs of his body, sent the message of Her presence to his nerve cells. His body turned without his willing it toward the lagoon where She waited.

Effortlessly he moved along, helped by the current, and, scorning the schools of small fish swimming by his side, he raced toward the herd.

If She recognized him, She did not show it, but She signaled to him nonetheless by raising one hand. As he moved toward Her, She swam out to meet him.

He went right up to Her and She drifted so that they touched, Her face on his shoulder, nuzzling. Then She ran Her fingers over his face and down both sides of his head, a knowing touch. As if satisfied, She moved away, but he followed. He touched Her shoulder. She did not turn, not at first. Then, after a long moment, She rolled and lay face up, almost motionless, looking up at him. The not-quite-scent struck him again, and all the males began to circle, slowly moving in. She flipped suddenly to an upright position, and a fury of bubbles cascaded from Her mouth. The males moved back, waiting.

She turned to him again, this time swimming sinuously to his side. He wanted to touch Her, but could not, some remnants of his humanity keeping him apart.

When he did not touch Her, She swam around him once more, trying to puzzle out the difference. She put Her face close to his, opening Her mouth as if to speak. It was dark red and cavernous, the teeth really a pearly ridge. Two bubbles formed at the corners of Her mouth, then slowly floated away. She had no tongue.

He tried to take Her hand and bring it to his lips, but She pulled away. So he put his hands on either side of Her face and brought Her head to his. She did not seem to know what to do, Her mouth remaining open all the while. He kissed Her gently on the open mouth and, getting no response, pressed harder.

Suddenly She fastened onto him, pressing Her body to his, Her cleft tail twining on each side of his thighs. The suction of Her mouth became irresistible. He felt as if his soul were being sucked out of his body, as if something inside were tearing. He tried desperately to pull back and could not. He opened his eyes briefly. Her eyes were sea-green, deep, fathomless, cold. Trying to draw away, he was drawn more closely to Her and, dying, he remembered land.

His body drifted up toward the light, turning slowly as it rose. The water bore it gently, making sure the limbs did not disgrace the death. His arms rose above his head and crossed slightly, as if in a dive; his legs trailed languidly behind.

She followed and after Her came the herd. It was a silent processional except for the murmurations of the sea.

When Eddystone's hands broke through the light, the herd rose into a great circle around it, their heads above the water's surface. One by one they touched his body curiously, seeming to support it. At last a ship found him. Only then did they dive, one after another. She was the last to leave. They did not look back.

The press conference was brief. The funeral service had been even briefer. Gabe had vetoed the idea of spreading Eddystone's ashes over the sea. "His body belongs to Hydrospace," Gabe had argued and, as Eddystone's oldest friend, his words were interpreted as Eddystone's wishes.

The medical people were wondering over the body now, with its strange webbings between the fingers and toes, and the violence with which the Breather valves had been torn from their moorings and set afloat inside Eddystone's body. None of it made any sense.

Gabe was trying to unriddle something more. The captain of the trawler that had picked up Eddystone's corpse some eight miles down the coast claimed he had found it because "a herd of dolphin had been holding it up." Scientifically that seemed highly unlikely. But, Gabe knew, there were many stories, many folktales, legends, *cousteaus* that claimed such things to be true. He could not, would not, let himself believe them.

It was Janney Hyatt at the press conference who posed the question Gabe had hoped not to have to answer.

"Do *you* consider Thomas Eddystone a hero?" she asked.

Gabe, conscious of the entire staff, both yellow and green smocks, behind him, took a moment before speaking. At last he said, "There are no heroes in Hydrospace. But if there were, Tommy Eddystone would be one. I want you all to remember this: he died for his dream, but the dream still lives. It lives Down Under. And we're going to make Tom Eddystone's dream come true. We're going to build cities and farms, a whole civilization, down under the sea. I think—no, I know—he would have liked it that way."

Out in the ocean, the herd members chased one another through the corridors of the sea. Mating season was over. The female drifted off alone. The bulls butted heads, then bodysurfed in pairs along the coast. Their lives were long, their memories short. They did not know how to mourn.

Antique Store Merman

Searching for teacups
Or out-of-date gems
In a back-alley store
On the banks of the Thames

I came on a merman
Adrift in a case,
The mummied remains
Of a submarine race.

Half carp and half monkey,
Half hokum, half dream.
I admired the craftsman
Who sewed such a seam.

Did the sailor who purchased
This hand-crafted prize
Believe in the seeming
And trust in the lies?

Did he show it to doctors?
Display it at fairs?
Or judging it barnum
Exile it upstairs

To swim in an ocean
Of dust and of dreams
Till seen by a poet
Who saw past its seams?

The Malaysian Mer

The shops were not noticeable from the main street and almost lost in the back-alley maze as well. But Mrs. Stambley was an expert at antiquing. A new city and a new back alley got up her hunting and gathering instincts, as she liked to tell her group at home. That this city was half a world away from her comfortable Salem, Massachusetts, home did not faze her. In England or America she guessed she knew how to look.

She had dozed in the sun as the boat made its way along the Thames. At her age naps had become important. Her head nodded peacefully under its covering of flowers draped on a wine-colored crown. She never even heard the tour guide's spiel. At Greenwich she had debarked meekly with the rest of the tourists, but she had easily slipped the leash of the guide, who took the rest of the pack up to check out Greenwich Mean Time. Instead, Mrs. Stambley, her large black leather pocketbook clutched in a sturdy gloved grip, had gone exploring on her own.

To the right of the harbor street was a group of shops and, she sensed, a back alley or two. The smell of it—sharp, mysterious, inviting—drew her in.

She ignored the main street and its big-windowed stores. A small cobbled path ran between two buildings and she slipped into it as comfortably as a foot into a well-worn slipper. There were several branchings, and Mrs. Stambley checked out each one with her watery blue eyes. Then she chose one. She knew it would be the right one. As she often said to her group at home, "I have a gift, a power. I am *never* wrong about it."

Here there were several small, dilapidated shops that seemed to edge one into the other. They had a worn look as if they had sat huddled together, the damp wind blowing off the river moldering their bones, while a bright new town had been built up around them. The windows were dirty, finger-streaked. Only the most intrepid shopper would find the way into them. There were no numbers on the doors.

The first store was full of maps. And if Mrs. Stambley hadn't already spent her paper allowance (she maintained separate monies for paper, gold, and oddities) on a rare chart of the McCodrun ancestry, she might have purchased a map of British waters that was decorated with tritons blowing "their wreathed horns" as the bent-over shopkeeper had quoted. She had been sorely tempted. Mrs. Stambley collected "objets d'mer," as she called them. Sea artifacts and antiquities. Sea magic was her specialty in the group. But the lineage of the Clan McCodrun— the reputed descendants of the selchies—had wiped out her comfortable paper account. And Mrs. Stambley, who was always precise in her reckonings, never spent more than her allotment. As the group's treasurer she had to keep the others in line. She could do no less for herself.

So she oohed and aahed at the map for the storekeeper's benefit and because it *was* quite beautiful and probably 17th century. She even managed to talk him down several pounds on the price, keeping her hand in as it were. But she left smiling her thanks. And he had been so impressed with the American lady's knowledge of the sea and its underwater folk that he smiled back even though she had bought nothing.

The next two shops were total wastes of time. One was full of reproductions and second-hand, badly painted china cups and cracked glassware. Mrs. Stambley sniffed as she left, muttering under her breath "Junk—spelled j-u-n-q-u-e," not even minding that the lady behind the counter heard her. The other store had been worse, a so-called craft shop full of handmade tea cosies and poorly crocheted afghans in simply appalling colors.

As she entered the fourth shop, Mrs. Stambley caught her breath. The smell was there, the smell of deep-sea magic. So deep and dark it might have been called up from the Mariana Trench. In all her years of hunting, she had never had such a find. She put her right hand over her heart and stumbled a bit, scuffing one of her sensible shoes. Then she straightened up and looked around.

The shop was a great deal longer than it was wide, with a staircase running up about halfway along the wall. The rest of the walls were lined with china cupboards in which Victorian and Edwardian cups and saucers were tastefully displayed. One in particular caught her eye because it had a Poseidon on the side. She walked over to look at it, but the magic smell did not come from there.

Books in stacks on the floor blocked her path, and she looked through a few to see what there was. She found an almost complete Britannica, the 1913 edition, missing only the thirteenth volume. There was a first edition of Fort's *Book of the Damned* and a dark grimoire so waterstained she could make out none of the spells. There were three paperback copies of *Folklore of the Sea*, a pleasant volume she had at home. And even the obscure *Melusine, Or the Mistress From the Sea* in both English and French.

She walked carefully around the books and looked for a moment at three glass cases containing fine replicas of early schooners, even down to the carved figureheads. One was of an Indian maiden, one an angel, one an unnamed muse with long, flowing hair. But she already had several such at home, her favorite a supposed replica of the legendary ship of the Flying Dutchman. Looking cost nothing, though, and so she looked for quite a while, giving herself time to become used to the odor of the deep magic.

She almost backed into a fourth case, and when she turned around, she got the shock of her life.

In a glass showcase with brass fittings, resting on two wooden holders, was a Malaysian mer.

She had read about them, of course, in the footnotes of obscure folklore journals and in a grimoire of specialized sea spells, but she had never in her wildest imaginings thought to see one. They were said to have disappeared totally.

They were not really mermen, of course. Rather, they were constructs made by Malaysian natives out of monkeys and fish. The Malaysians killed the monkeys, cut off the top half, from the navel up, and sewed on a fish tail. The mummified remains were then sold to innocent British tars in Victorian times. The natives had called the mummies mermen and the young sailors believed them, brought the mers home and gave them to loved ones.

And here, resting on its wooden stands, was a particularly horrible example of one, probably rescued from an attic where it had lain all these years, dust-covered, rotting.

It was gray-green, with gray more predominant, and so skeletal that its rib cage reminded Mrs. Stambley of the pictures of starving children in Africa. Its arms were held stiffly in front as if it were doing an out-of-water dog paddle. The grimacing face, big-lipped, big-eared, stared out at her in horror. She could not see the stitches that held the monkey half to the fish.

"I see you like our mer," came a voice from behind her, but Mrs. Stambley did not turn. She simply could not take her eyes from the grotesque mummy in the glass and brass case.

"A Malaysian mer," Mrs. Stambley whispered. One part of her noticed the price sticker on the side of the glass—three hundred pounds. Six hundred American dollars. It was more than she had with her . . . but . . .

"You know what it is, then," the voice went on. "That is too bad. Too bad."

The mer blinked its lashless lids and turned its head. Its eyes were entirely black, without irises. When it rolled its lips back, it showed sharp yellow-gray teeth. It had no tongue.

Mrs. Stambley tried to look away and could not. Instead she felt herself being drawn down, down, down into the black deeps of those eyes.

"That really is *too* bad," came the voice again, but now it was very far away and receding quickly.

Mrs. Stambley tried to open her mouth to scream, but only bubbles came out. All around her it was dark and cold and wet, and still she was pulled downward until she landed, with a jarring thud, on a sandy floor. She stood, brushed her skirts down, and settled her hat back on her head. Then, as she placed her pocketbook firmly under one arm, she felt a grip on her ankle, as if seaweed wanted to root her to that spot. She started to struggle against it when a change in the current against her face forced her to look up.

The mer was swimming toward her, lazily, as if it had all the time in the world to reach her.

She stopped wasting her strength in fighting the seaweed manacle, and instead cautiously fingered open her pocketbook. All the while she watched the mer, which had already halved the distance between them. Its mouth was opening and closing with terrifying snaps. Its bony fingers, with the opaque webbings, seemed to reach out for her. Its monkey face grinned. Behind it was a dark, roiling wake.

The water swirled about Mrs. Stambley, picking at her skirt, flipping the hem to show her slip. Above the swimming mer, high above, she could see the darker shadows of circling sharks waiting for what the mer would leave them. But even they feared to come any closer while he was on the hunt.

And then he was close enough so that she could see the hollow of his mouth, the scissored teeth, the black nails, the angry pulsing beat of the webbings. The sound he made came to her through the filtering of the water. It was like the groans and creaks of a sinking ship.

Her hand was inside the pocketbook now, fingers closing on the wallet and poking into the change purse for the wren feathers she kept there. She grabbed them up and held them before her. They were air magic, stronger than that of the sea, and blessed in church. It was luck against seafolk. Her hand trembled only slightly. She spoke a word of power that was washed from her lips into the troubled water.

For a moment the mer stopped, holding his gray hands before his face.

The seaweed around Mrs. Stambley's ankle slithered away. She kicked her foot out and found she was free.

But above a Great White Shark turned suddenly, sending a wash of new water across Mrs. Stambley's front. The tiny feathers broke and she had to let them go. They floated past the mer and were gone.

He put down his hands, gave the monkey grin at her again, and resumed swimming. But she knew—as he did—that he was not immune to her knowledge. It gave her some slight hope.

Her hand went back into her purse and found the zippered pocket. She unzipped it and drew out seven small bones, taken from a male horseshoe crab found on the Elizabeth Islands off the coast near New Bedford. They were strong sea magic and she counted heavily on them. She wrapped her fingers around the seven, held them first to her breast, then to her forehead, then flung them at the mer.

The bones sailed between them and in the filtered light seemed to dance and grow and change and cling together at last into a maze.

Mrs. Stambley kicked her feet, sending up a trough of bubbles, and, holding her hat with one hand, her purse with the other, eeled into the bone-maze. She knew that it would hold for only a minute or two at best.

Behind her she could hear the hunting cry of the mer as it searched for a way in. She ignored it and kicked her feet in a steady rhythm, propelling herself into the heart of the maze. Going in was always easier than coming out. Her bubble trail would lead the mer through once he found the entrance. For now she could still hear him knocking against the walls.

Her purse held one last bit of magic. It was a knife that had been given up by the sea, left on a beach on the North Shore, near Rockport. It had a black handle with a guard and she had mounted a silver coin on its haft.

The seawater laid shifting patterns on the blade that looked now like fire, now like air, the calligraphy of power. Mrs. Stambley knew better than to try to read it. Instead she turned toward the passage where the mer would have to appear. The knife in her right hand, her hat askew, the purse locked under her left arm, Mrs. Stambley guessed she did not look like a seasoned fighter. But in magic, as any good witch knew, *seeming* was all important. And she was not about to give up.

"Great Lir," she spoke, and her human tongue added extra urgency to the bubbles which flowered from her mouth. "Bull-roarer Poseidon, spear-thrower Neptune, mighty Njord, shrewish Ran, cleft-tailed Dagon, hold me safe in the green palms of your hands. Bring me safely from the sea. And when I am home, I will gift you and yours."

From somewhere near an animal called, a bull, a horse, a great sea serpent. It was her answer. In moments she would know what it meant. She put her right hand with the knife behind her and waited.

The water in the maze began to churn angrily and the mer came around the final turning. Seeing Mrs. Stambley backed against the flimsy wall, he laughed. The laugh cascaded out of his mouth in a torrent of bubbles. Their popping made a peculiar punctuation to his mirth. Then he showed his horrible teeth once again, swung his tail to propel himself forward, and moved in for the kill.

Mrs. Stambley kept the knife hidden until the very last moment. And then, as the mer's skeletal arms reached out for her, as the fingers of his hands actually pressed against her neck, and his sharp incisors began to bear down on her throat, she whipped her arms around and slashed at his side. He drew back in pain, and then she knifed him again, as expertly as if she were filleting a fish. He arched his back, opened his mouth in a silent scream of bubbles, and rose slowly toward the white light of the surface.

The maze vanished. Mrs. Stambley stuffed the knife back into her purse, then put her hands over her head, and rose too, leaving a trail of bubbles as dark as blood behind.

"*Too* bad," the voice was finishing.

Mrs. Stambley turned around and smiled blandly, patting her hat into place. "Yes, I know," she said. "It's too bad it is in such condition. For three hundred pounds, I would want something a bit better cared for."

She stepped aside.

The shopkeeper, a wizened, painted old lady with a webbing between her second and third fingers, breathed in sharply. In the showcase, the mummied mer had tipped over on its back. Along one side was a deep, slashing wound. The chest cavity was hollow. It stank. Under the body were seven small knobby sticks that looked surprisingly like bones.

"Yes," Mrs. Stambley continued, not bothering to apologize

for her hasty exit, "rather poor condition. Shocking what some folk will try to palm off on tourists. Luckily I know better." She exited through the front door and was relieved to find that the sun lit the alleyway. She put her hand to her ample bosom and breathed deeply.

"Wait, just wait until I tell the group," she said aloud. Then she threaded her way back to the main street where the other tourists and their guide were coming down the hill. Mrs. Stambley walked briskly toward them, straightening her hat once again and smiling. Not even the thought of the lost triton map could dampen her spirits. The look of surprise on the face of that old witch of a shopkeeper had been worth the scare. Only what gift could she give to the gods that would be good enough? It was a thought that she could puzzle over happily all the way home.

Metamorphosis

I saw a sailor once
shed his skin
as quickly as a crab
sloughs its shell.
He danced alone,
easy in his bones,
amid the coral memories
of his sunken ship.
When he opened his mouth
little colored fish
swam in and out,
avoiding his brittle teeth,
his stripped and shining jaw.
They were as quick and bright
as laughter,
running their zigzag course
through the silent syncopation
of the sea.

JANE YOLEN is one of today's most versatile and distinguished writers of books for young readers, equally acclaimed for her poetry, her humorous novels, picture book texts, comic verse, serious biographies and novels for young adults, and her collections of original fantasies and fairytales. Myth is at the center of many of her writings, particularly of her short fantasies, some of which have been described by critics as "modern classics." Married and the mother of three children, Ms. Yolen lives in western Massachusetts.

DAVID WIESNER studied at the Rhode Island School of Design. He is the illustrator of several books for children and his paintings have been exhibited in various New York galleries as well as in the Metropolitan Museum of Art. Mr. Wiesner lives and works in New York City.